SHAYNE PRESCOTT

Copyright © 2022 by Shayne Prescott

All rights reserved. Names, characters and incidents depicted in this book are products of the author's imagination or are used fictitiously. Any resemblance to actual events, locales, organizations, or persons, living or dead, is entirely coincidental and beyond the intent of the author or the publisher. No part of this book may be reproduced or shared by any electronic or mechanical means, including but not limited to printing, file sharing, and email, without prior written permission from the author.

Cover design by Get Covers.

Editing by Aspen Tree E.A.S.

SPARTAKITTAH PRESS

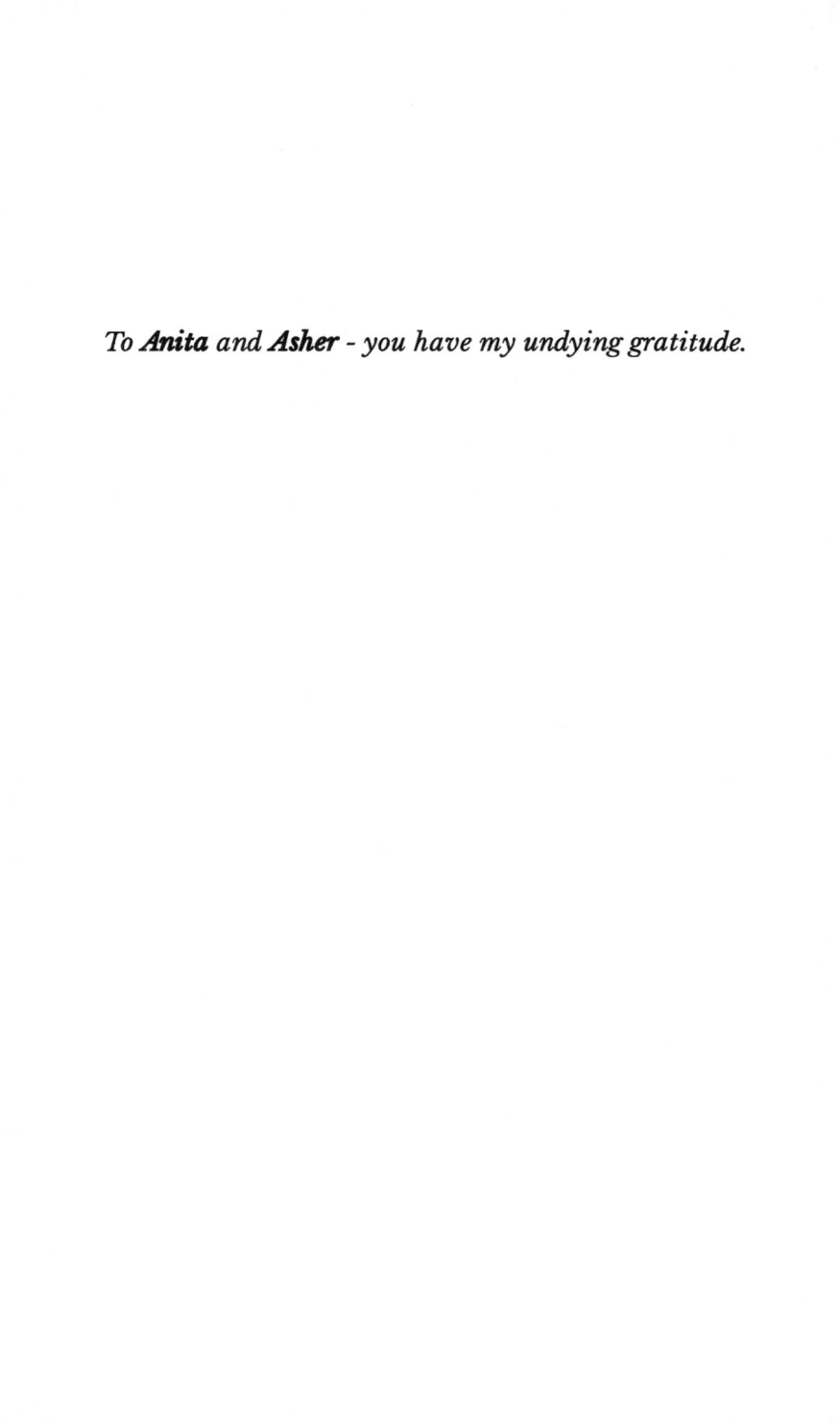

*To **Anita** and **Asher** - you have my undying gratitude.*

At Roseden University, students entering their first year of study are referred to as "Frosh", not "Freshmen" as the latter term is not gender-inclusive. All other typical years of study (Sophomore, Junior, Senior) remain the same.

The Us Against the World playlist

1. "I won't Give Up" - Jason Mraz
2. "What Hurts the Most" - Rascal Flatts
3. "My Life is Going on" - Cecilia Krull
4. "Chasing Cars" - Snow Patrol
5. "Stereo Hearts" - Gym Class Hereos ft Adam Levine
6. "Say Something" - A Great Big World ft. Christine Aguilera
7. "It's Not Just Me" - Rascal Flatts
8. "You and Me" - Lifehouse
9. "Soldier" - Gavin DeGraw
10. "You Wanted More" - Tonic
11. "Come Home" - OneRepublic
12. "Kiss Me Slowly" - Parachute
13. "Just a Kiss" - Lady A
14. "Without You Here" - The Goo Goo Dolls
15. "Start of Something Good" - Daughtry
16. "Shouldn't Be Good in Goodbye" - Jason Walker
17. "You're Beautiful" - Chester See
18. "Fade into Me" - David Cook
19. "Just So you Know" - Jesse McCartney
20. "Chances" - Five for Fighting
21. "Come Wake Me Up" - Rascal Flatts
22. "Yours to Hold" - Skillet
23. "Between the Raindrops" - Lifehouse ft. Natasha Bedingfield
24. "Wait for Me" - Theory of a Deadman
25. "Your Arms Feel Like Home" - 3 Doors Down

Click Me with your Phone to Open Spotify Playlist

Please be advised that this book contains some derogatory language (LGBTQIA+).

Contents

1. Theo	1
2. Owen	12
3. Theo	18
4. Owen	24
5. Theo	37
6. Owen	50
7. Theo	61
8. Owen	72
9. Theo	85
10. Owen	99
11. Theo	112
12. Owen	122
13. Theo	133
14. Owen	143
15. Theo	155
16. Owen	164
17. Theo	174
18. Owen	186

19. Theo	197
20. Owen	209
21. Theo	220
22. Owen	231
Epilogue - Theo	241
Also By Shayne Prescott	249
About Shayne	250

1

Theo

"Talk about awkward. You okay, Theo?"

The door had just barely closed on my parents' asses as they left my dorm room at Roseden University, and their exit found me banging my head against my desk. Despite my many protests, my parents had told my new roommate, Harvard "call me Harv" Bates, why they fully expected me to be on the receiving end of bullying. "Yeah," I finally ventured. "I'm sorry for them."

"Don't be. They obviously meant well. I'm amazed you convinced them to leave you behind."

Persuading my parents to go home to New Hampshire had taken all of my wits and much of my patience. How many more times could Mom come back into the room to check "just one more thing"? Pinching my nose to ward off an impending migraine, she finally seemed to get the hint and left once and for all. The sight of a groundhog over in Punxsutawney meant spring semester at the all-male liberal arts university had started, but I hadn't been on campus before this semester.

"Are you going to be okay?" Harv asked, and I looked up to find sincere, if concerned, eyes looking me over.

I gave him a valiant smile. "I'm a pipsqueak, but I'm fierce. Or at least that's what I keep telling myself." Harv grinned at me. "I appreciate you sitting there, absorbing that all without running like hell."

His smile faded. "Why would I run? Just because you've been through a lot? What kind of friend would that make me?"

"Friends?" My brows furrowed.

"I know, it's early yet, but we're going to be roommates, right? Friends would be logical."

I tilted my head before finally nodding. He was right. Of course he was right. "I'm good with that. I need to go to the bookstore though to get my books. How about you?"

"I'm good. Only needed one book; the rest of mine are eBooks. Hallelujah for that. Where's a Jesus emoji when you need one?"

"Oh my God, Harv, you're too much." I laughed and rose to my feet. Things were going well with him, though they almost seemed too easy. Or maybe I was just that jaded. The joy slid from my body, replaced by an almost resigned feeling.

With hunched shoulders and a wave at Harv, I ventured out of our dorm room in Tucker Hall, one of the two Frosh-only dorms here at RU, and headed on my way. When I finally reached the campus bookstore, it was virtually empty, and I breathed a sigh of relief, though a staffer quickly came to greet me. Owen, according to his name tag, tall and Black, had a build like a football player.

A stunning individual, it took all of my willpower to keep my jaw from hitting the ground.

"Hi! Do you need help finding your books?" My books, my brain, my capacity to speak...

"Y-yes." My tongue tangled like when I was a kid, when I'd had a mouth full of Gobstoppers and couldn't manage any words. I bet I looked really intelligent.

Owen grinned at me, either oblivious or nonplussed by my brainless moments. "Do you have your class schedule? I'll need that to find your books."

"Sure do," I confirmed. I handed him my class list and he looked it over, nodding quietly to himself before suddenly grinning even wider at me.

"You're in my Spanish class. But I don't remember seeing you in the fall semester?"

"I took the fall semester online, back home in New Hampshire." Before he could ask why — I could see the curiosity on his chiseled face — I explained. "I had surgery early in the year; it made more sense to be home, rather than recovering here." Smooth, Theo, so smooth. Why don't you tell him about the time you tripped and skinned both knees while you're at it?

Owen nodded. "I totally get that. So since you've got Spanish covered, it'll just be the other four classes?"

"Yeah. Take all my money," I groused, and he laughed, which made my stomach do a little flip-flop. I fought the urge to groan. I needed to get over myself. I didn't know this guy, and despite him looking damn good, I shouldn't have been swooning.

Owen went off to search the stacks for the books, while I decided to pick up some more highlighters. I'd brought some from home, but given the current state of my Spanish book, it would take me no time at all before those were dried up and in need of replacements. Finding a five-pack of assorted colors, I made a happy little noise and snatched them up, coming back to the book section just as Owen approached with a thick stack of books.

"Oh God. How am I going to get all of those back to my dorm?" Yes, Theo, complain to the handsome man about your own ineptitude.

Owen peeked around the books to peer down at me. "You didn't bring a backpack?" I shook my head morosely. "Two options. You can either buy a Roseden one, or if you've got one back in your room, I can set the books aside while you go grab it."

"Can you really set them aside?" Owen nodded. "Okay, thanks! I'll get back here as fast as I can."

"Don't rush," Owen assured me with a dazzling smile. "It's been slow. More professors are going for online textbooks instead of the physical ones."

I hazarded a glance at my stack. "Not mine, it seems." Owen winked at me and my stomach fluttered again. I started towards the door, then remembered the highlighters in my hand. Turning, I placed them beside my texts. "I'll pay for those, too, when I come back." Owen gave me a friendly wave, and then I was off, back to Tucker Hall.

It wasn't long before I was back inside the dorm, sweating slightly from the exertion of jogging up the stairs. "You're back quick...and where are your books?"

"Forgot my backpack," I answered as I went into my closet, burrowing around until I emerged triumphantly with the oversized bag. "The sales dude offered to hold my books aside until I got back."

"That's cool." Harv paused. "He didn't give you any trouble, did he?"

"Why would he?"

"What your parents were saying."

I sighed, long and loud. "My parents tend to worry too much. Please don't let them get in your head like they've gotten in mine. I don't need you worrying about things I'm already worrying about. Let me get my books from the cutie in the bookstore, and then we can talk more, okay?"

"Cutie in the bookstore" he mouthed at me before he nodded and gave me a bit of a grin. The heat rose to my face but I turned away, throwing the backpack over my shoulder and moving to exit the dorm room, back to the bookstore.

It took me a few minutes, because while I'm not flabby by any stretch, I lacked the definition of my new friend in the bookstore. When I got inside, I found him leaning against the counter by the register, and I sucked in a quick breath. He really was gorgeous, with big brown eyes and long lashes. He was an immense specimen of a man. Thick arms visible even under the Roseden hoodie he wore, and khakis that loved him as much as I loved them on him. "Hi, Owen," I said breathlessly.

"Hi, Theo," he replied, and when I gaped at him, he smiled. "Your name was on your class list." He'd noticed my name?? "I hope you don't mind, I grabbed you another package of highlighters; they're buy one get one free this week."

I nodded dumbly, and as he rang the lot up, I winced when the total ended up over three hundred dollars. I pulled out my debit card and handed it over to Owen to charge, and I could have sworn he looked at it wistfully, but it had to have been my imagination. When I pulled my backpack off my shoulder, Owen helped me load it up, and I made an "oooof" noise when I put it back on.

"You okay?" His eyes flashed with concern, and the thought that this beautiful stranger would care that much damn near undid me.

"Yeah, I'm just out of shape," I replied with a laughing huff. Could he not see the pudge around my middle? A blessing for me if he somehow couldn't.

"You should come work out with me some time," Owen offered, and though I raised an eyebrow, he continued. "I usually work out with the rest of the lacrosse team. Have you ever played?"

I shook my head quickly. "I'm familiar with the sport, but I didn't play anything when I was growing up."

"Ah well. I suppose I'll see you on Friday for Intensive Spanish II."

"Yeah, I guess you will," I answered, still in a bit of wonder that he'd want to see me again. "Nice meeting you, Owen."

"Same, Theo. Have a good rest of your move-in day. Try to relax before the chaos begins on Friday."

I snorted, mostly to myself. Calling Friday chaotic? Probably the understatement of the year. I shot him a very shy smile before exiting the bookstore and heading back to Tucker Hall, taking my time and observing my surroundings.

It was a chilly afternoon, but the Endless Mountains were still visible in the distance. Maybe I could join a hiking club and trek those peaks this term? That would certainly get me in shape.

Eventually, I was using my thumbprint to get inside the dorm, very grateful that Harv and I were on the second floor and not the fourth. Maybe those mountains would have to wait if I was this much out of breath already. Returning to our room, I found Harv where I left him — sitting backwards in his desk chair, tapping away at his laptop.

"Hey," I greeted him, as I closed the door behind me and moved to dump the books on my desk.

Harv turned around to face me. "Hey yourself. So how was the cutie? Does that mean you're gay? Do we need a rule about bringing boys back to the room?"

There went my face warming again even as I flipped Harv off. "Cutie was cute. His name is Owen. He plays lacrosse and is in my Spanish class."

Sculpted eyebrows arched high in the air. "Damn, that's a lot of intel to gather in such a short time. You must really like this guy."

I tried like hell to deny that initial attraction, shaking my head fiercely, but I don't know if I was believable. "He offered up all of that on his own. I wasn't going fishing for info. I wouldn't have minded it, but a guy like that? He's totally out of my league, and besides, he's probably straight. Athletes usually are."

"Well, prepare yourself. I just pulled up FisherFriends and searched up the Pride Council page, and one of its members is Ethan Kim. That name sound familiar to you at all?" I shook my head. "He's a senior and student body vice president. He's also the star running back of the Fighting Fishers football team. And he's been posting to the others on the page about how his *boyfriend*, Joshua, has been recovering from his broken leg."

For the second time in less than an hour, I found myself gaping, eyes wide. An out athlete? And in such a prominent role, at that? Maybe fate was telling me that this school experience wasn't going to be so bad after all. "It sounds like I need to get involved with Pride Council. I'll check it out when I get on my laptop."

"I direct messaged you the link to their FisherFriends page. That should help. And if you join, maybe I will join you."

"Oh, do they accept allies?"

"Yeah," Harv answered quickly. Almost too quickly, if I was being honest with myself. But Harv couldn't be gay too, could he? He wasn't setting off my gaydar at all, especially not with the calendar above his desk of women in skimpy swimsuits. Unless he was still very much in the closet? I shook my head. It wasn't my place to push that button or yank him out of the closet if that's where he needed to be.

Rather than go there, I decided to test Harv's google-fu. "Hey, Harv, do they have the bookstore staff on the school website? Maybe we can get a last name for Owen and stalk him on FisherFriends?"

My roommate laughed at me. "Or we can look at the lacrosse page. That'll tell us where he's from, his height and weight. Oh! And what position he plays. Not that I know much about lacrosse, except it's supposed to be like hockey on grass. Fast and fierce. You need to be tough like a hockey player to be good."

"He looked tough. I could see muscles through his hoodie." Giving Harv a conspiratorial grin, I continued. "Honestly, I'm surprised there wasn't a little circle of drool beneath me when I left. He was *that* hot."

"Owen sounds very friendly. Though maybe he has to be for his job." That made me pause. Maybe Owen was always as forthcoming with information about himself and his school activities as he'd been with me?

"Oh, don't pout. It's not a good look on you."

I flicked him the bird, tugging a laugh out of Harv in the process. "So what's his last name?"

"Lewis. He's from Owensboro, Kentucky. Ooooh...did he have a nice drawl? Did he say y'all?"

I cocked my head slightly, trying to cling onto the memory before it completely escaped my mind. "I...don't think so? There was definitely a hint of a drawl, but it wasn't like 'oh my god' in your face or anything."

Harv actually looked disappointed. "Well, for a guy, he's attractive. Nice eyes though, I bet you noticed those."

"You bet I did," I answered quickly, face heating up at how embarrassingly overboard I was about this still virtual stranger. "His smile though...it's nice, but it doesn't quite reach his eyes."

He gazed at me thoughtfully. "He's probably just a private person despite his seeming infodump on you."

I shrugged. "Your guess is as good as mine. And I doubt I'll find out much more. We may be in the same Spanish class, but that doesn't mean he'd pay me any mind. Maybe a friendly hello if he's that kind of guy, but just selling books to a guy does not a relationship make."

"No, and here's another potential bubble burster for you: he's a junior."

"I think I was right the first time when I said he was way out of my league," I indicated to Harv, thinking that instead of dreaming of said junior, I needed to be aiming for something more attainable, like a decent enough looking frosh. "I think going to Pride Council will definitely be a good idea. I should be able to meet other single gay guys."

"You never know, but odds are better there," Harv conceded.

I sighed and flopped on my back, grabbing my stuffed bear made out of my grandpa's favorite Hawaiian shirt. "Maybe I should have just gone to a more local liberal arts school, been in more 'normal' surroundings. Maybe then I wouldn't feel so in over my head."

"Relax." He came closer to my bunk, patting me on the arm. "We haven't even started classes yet. Things will get better."

I hoped Harv was right.

2

Owen

"So I met the cutest little frosh in the bookstore today."

Brent Larsen, my longtime roommate, paused his game to peer at me as I changed out of my work clothes. "Where's he fit on your 'I would bang him' scale?"

"Oh, I would totally bang him," I replied as I carefully hung my khakis up on their hanger. "Problem is, I don't know if he plays on my team or yours. All the cute guys are usually gay, but..."

"I'm not," Brent teased, and I snorted loudly in his direction.

"Face it, Brent. You secretly dig my ass, and that's why we've been roommates since our frosh year. Misha is totally just a beard," I swore, and this time, he was the one snorting.

"If she heard you say that..." he started as he shook his head.

"I see there's no denial about digging my ass, just worries about how Misha would react," I continued to tease, and this time he flipped me off.

"Ass."

"Yes, we've established you like mine." I moved to boot up my ancient, school-provided laptop, hoping to check out FisherFriends to see if I could find Theo on there at all. Not that I was going to stalk him or anything. I just wanted to learn more about him. There was nothing wrong with that, right?

"Tell me about this frosh you met."

"Short. Especially compared to me." At nearly six feet six inches, I towered over even six foot tall Brent, so Theo must have been especially short. "I'd guess around five-eight or so? Not chubby, but..." It took me a moment while I searched for the perfect word. "Fluffy. Carrying a bit of extra weight, but it doesn't look bad on him?"

"Not like weight has ever made a difference to you," Brent noted. "Mary-Ellen was the epitome of a fat-bottomed girl."

I groaned. "Must we talk about her? It's been two years and I still have regrets."

"That you didn't see her for the user she was sooner than you did?" I nodded. "You live and learn. You were only nineteen. Speaking of, any ideas how old your frosh is? Does he have a name you know of?"

"Theo. Theo Carter. Given that he's a frosh, I'd guess eighteen or nineteen. He *is* in my Spanish class, though."

"You didn't mention him before though."

"He wasn't on campus last semester. Something about surgery. He moved around just fine, so whatever it was couldn't have been too horribly serious," I mused, finally getting FisherFriends up on the laptop and searching for his name. "Private page, figures. Looks like he's using a high school class photo for his FisherFriends profile photo."

Brent pulled himself out of his bean bag chair to venture over to my desk, peering over my shoulder to gaze at Theo. "Nice smile, but I'm guessing you already noticed that."

"Oh, I did," I confirmed. "Shy little smile most of the time, but I got a few true smiles out of him."

Brent patted me on the back then moved to flop back in his bean bag chair, this time turning it to face me. "That's got to be hard for him though, coming to school for the spring semester after missing the fall. Trying to make friends, trying to find his way around campus. I'm glad we had each other to get lost with."

Closing my eyes, I thought back to our frosh year and how scared I was. Away from Kentucky for maybe the fourth time in my life, Roseden was all that I had. No home to go back to, even during breaks. No family that I could send report cards back to. "I'm so glad I had you," I murmured.

"Mutual, my friend," Brent told me. "I know your childhood was rough. I'm just glad you made it here. And hey, you met me and we both know how awesome I am, so it was all worth it in the end, right?"

I drew my eyes open to roll them in his direction. "I think you're really overestimating how much I like you, but I'm glad I'm here in spite of that..." I trailed off, finding words failing me as they often did in this type of situation. I wasn't comfortable talking about my childhood. It made my skin feel tight. I had little doubt it affected the way I interacted with people, from my lacrosse teammates to potential friends or lovers. "Open tryouts coming up in the next several weeks. I still can't believe you'd never played before you tried out with me frosh year."

Brent smirked in my direction. "What can I say? I'm good at handling my stick." I snorted back a laugh, and Brent's smirk grew wider. "Let us not forget my skills in cradling my balls."

I finally barked out a laugh, doubling over at the desk before shaking my head. "It's a good team, a good family we have." Brent looked dubious but didn't argue. "Maybe it doesn't feel that way to you, but remember, sports has long been the only family I've ever had. And yeah, I always have to prove my worth to keep my place in the family, but at least there's a spot for me in the meanwhile."

"You shouldn't have to prove yourself," Brent replied quietly. "Any family would be lucky to have you."

"Yeah, we see how well *that* has worked out for me, right?" I countered, muscles tightening in frustration.

Brent put his hand up in an "I mean no harm" gesture and I sighed softly, some of my frustration seeping away. It wasn't his fault he didn't truly understand what my life was like. He'd tried his best to be there for me, even convincing his parents to invite me to their home in DC for the holidays. He said a family would be lucky to have me, but I was lucky to have *him*. "What are you going to do about Theo?"

"What can I do?" I asked.

"Sit near him in your Spanish class? Maybe offer him a tour of campus?" Brent proposed, and I just gazed at him thoughtfully.

"Mighty presumptuous of you to even assume he plays for my team," I reminded Brent. "But let's say he does. What makes you think he'd want to get to know *me* better?"

"Did he run away screaming from you in the bookstore? Did he flirt with you at all?"

Gnawing on my lip, I tried to analyze that conversation with Theo from a different vantage point. Was it possible he flirted with me? His eyes were on me, sure, but I'd assumed he'd never seen a big Black man before. "Maybe?" I finally offered.

"Were *you* flirting with him?"

"Of course, dorkbreath." I stuck my tongue out at him, and he made a point of lewdly licking his lips back at me, making me double over in laughter again. "Okay, stop that." Chuckling, it took me a moment to get my wits fully together. "I flirt with all the cute guys, though I'm subtle about it, or try to be. I don't want someone trying to fight me because they're offended by my interest."

"So what made him special?"

That gave me pause. "He was shy yet excited all rolled up into one endearing little ball. I feel like I could have offered him a hug and he would have just snuggled up in my arms and tucked in under my chin and fit there, y'know?"

"So it's mostly physical, but you dug his personality too. That's promising."

I nodded after a moment. "I wasn't looking for anyone though. And if this turns into nothing, which it probably will, then it's no big deal. He was cute. End of."

Brent rolled his eyes at me but didn't press any further.

3

Thea

"How are you feeling about the semester so far?"

I looked up from my laptop to gaze in Harv's direction, quirking a smile at him and replying. "Not bad. Better than my parents expected, for sure. No one is bothering me, no one has even mentioned that stupid TV show. I'm not rolling in friends; in fact, I've only got you, but I'm fine with that. I'm used to fending for myself."

"You've definitely got me," Harv assured me. "But no one has tried to get to know you better? Even Owen from the bookstore?"

"Nope," I confirmed. "I've seen him in class; he usually sits in the middle of the room while I sit in the back. But he hasn't approached me at all. So it goes. Like I said, I'm used to fending for myself."

"Why is that?"

"Because people inherently are...less than kind to me. I don't know if it's just a society-wide transphobia or if it's me or what, but when I encounter people, they either have rude things to say, or they're trying to take advantage of me." I shrugged, turning back towards my laptop, not wanting to let him see how much this line of conversation bothered me.

"When you say they take advantage of you..."

"That's exactly what I mean," I answered shortly. "Whether it's members of the football team trying to convince me that they're gay when really they just want to haze me, or people who tried to befriend me to get on the TV show, I'm over it. I'm over people in general, to be honest."

"Dare I ask how they tried to haze you?" he ventured, and I almost shook my head at him, but I decided to answer.

"Let's just suffice it to say they thought it would be fun to try and convince me they were genuinely interested in me, when they really thought it would be funny to try and get down my pants. I guess they figured I'd be easier than a girl? Dude only found out that I've got very bony knees, and I spent the rest of that school year taking online classes."

"So they tried to rape you," Harv spat out.

I nodded, not really wanting to talk about it further, and thankfully, Harv seemed to sense that.

"What about Owen?"

"What about him?" I countered.

"Didn't you want to try and get to know him better?" he asked, and I shrugged at him.

"Yeah but...I can't make him be interested in me. And like I told you after I got back from the bookstore that day, he's out of my league." I paused, changing the topic on him. "Pride Council was good though."

"Yeah, it was," he agreed. "Even though they did say people were missing, that was a fun crowd. It was nice to meet Ethan and his boyfriend Joshua."

I nodded, finally relaxing a little bit. "I liked Joshua. He's so smart; that was a bit intimidating at first, but he's so easy going that it was impossible not to like him."

"I thought maybe you'd check out some of the single guys there."

I'd be lying if I told him I hadn't thought about it, but..."I'm mostly in the look don't touch camp right now. Mostly because I don't want to be touched."

"After what you mentioned earlier, I can understand that."

I frowned again, but facing my laptop, I hoped he didn't notice. "Sebi was fun," I tried. "I've never met anyone that *flamboyant* before. But that fedora did look fabulous on him."

Something bounced off my head, and turning, I found Harv had a stack of mini-erasers in his hand, ready to pelt at me. "I bet he'd be a trip at a Pride Parade."

I flung the eraser back at him and Harv's only response was to give me a smirk. "I've never been to one. I should, but again, it's the whole not fitting in thing."

"I think you'd fit in at a Pride Parade," Harv countered. "But I mean your parents are supportive, right? Yeah, they put you on that show, but that wasn't to embarrass you or anything; they thought it would be good for you."

"Yeah, so good for me." I rolled my eyes.

"Twenty-twenty hindsight," he murmured. "How could they know it would get you ostracized, would make for fake friends, and would otherwise make you miserable? At least you got the royalties from it; that counts for something, right?"

"Yeah," I sighed. "It means I was able to go here when otherwise I would have had to hope for a scholarship. And I know that they meet everyone's needs one way or another, but I don't think I could handle having to go to classes and find time to do work study, y'know? The thing of it is, my parents failed me big time. They should have known better than to put me in that position. I think despite how much I love them, there's a part of me that still resents them." The familiar sting in my eyes and thickness in my throat made me want to stop this conversation. But Harv seemed genuine, and in spite of my past, I desperately wanted a friend.

"Yeah, I get it. I'm lucky that with my family, that'll never be an issue. Course, sometimes I think I'd rather have a different family with less money and less stress."

I gave Harv a sad smile. His parents had named him Harvard with the expectation that their one and only would go to that school. Though Roseden was a top notch liberal arts university, it was no Harvard, and Harv's parents constantly expressed their disappointment in his choice. "For what it's worth, I'm glad you're here."

He gave me a brilliant smile. "I'm glad we've gotten to know each other. Though I'll readily admit, after last semester's disaster of a rooming situation, they asked me if I'd be okay with a trans roommate. I didn't see any issue. You may have been assigned female at birth, but you're a guy, and that's all that matters to me. About the only thing that makes you a little different is you've still got some gender dysphoria."

I nodded; he was absolutely right about that. I got uncomfortable when it came to undressing around other people, Harv included, and usually ducked into my closet when it came to changing out of my boxers. My discomfort with my body was pretty plain if even Harv could see it. My life would have been so much easier if I had been just given the right body at birth instead of this one.

Maybe I should have been annoyed at the school about presenting me to Harv before I even got to meet him, but I got a good roommate out of the deal, so it worked out for me.

"Are you going to go to the next Pride Council gathering?"

Smiling, I nodded. "I'm planning on it, how about you?"

"I think so. You're not the only one short on friends. And as we said, they're a good bunch of guys."

"Exactly," I agreed. "And who knows, maybe as I get more comfortable here, I'll get past looking at the eye candy and actually try and ask someone out. Though hopefully by that point I'll be more familiar with campus. Seeing as how at this point my full experience is the triangle of dorm, lecture hall, cafeteria."

"You've got to admit, that's a good triangle, but yeah, I'd take you out on a tour now if you weren't eyeballs deep in homework." I nodded sadly. "Maybe later?"

"Later could work. I know there's a lot of stuff here, because it said so on the school website, but it's different when you see stuff first hand."

"Alright. I'll let you get back to your homework now. Poke me if you need anything."

"I could just find an eraser to throw," I teased and he laughed.

I definitely had a good roommate situation going on.

4
Owen

Taking a shower after getting off from work had helped me prepare mentally for my Friday classload, but it didn't prepare me for what I found in my Intensive Spanish classroom. In the back, where the cute frosh usually sat, was a small crowd of people, and I could hear raised voices, even from the doorway.

Curiosity got the better of me. My heart sank when I noted that it was one of my young teammates who was causing the disturbance — and wee Theo was the one taking the heat. "Is there a problem, y'all?" I questioned as I smoothly slid into the seat beside Theo, raising an eyebrow at Aaron Callahan, the sophomore who seemed to be the ringleader of this nonsense.

"We have a girl in our midst, Owen," Aaron informed me, and when I raised my eyebrow at him, he pointed at Theo. "She was on a TV series about being transgender. She's not really a guy. She doesn't belong here."

I looked Theo up and down before giving Aaron a reproachful look. "He looks male to me."

The sophomore made a noise of disgust and repeated his earlier words. "She doesn't belong here."

Briefly, I wondered if there was something more to Aaron's attitude problem about Theo, but I wisely kept that question to myself and instead told him, "Class is about to begin." He narrowed his eyes at me, but I continued. "Shouldn't you get to your seats?"

"You gonna stay here and guard the girl?" he spat before he stalked away, his frosh flunkies trailing behind him like puppies.

When I turned to face Theo, I found his eyes closed, and his body trembled a little. Quietly, I shifted a hand to rest it on his knee, and though he jumped slightly, the tremor also went away. "Thank you," he eventually whispered, and I gave his knee a squeeze.

"Not a problem," I assured him in just as soft a voice. "I'm sorry they were bothering you. I'll have a talk with Coach about that. But it might be a bit. Our season doesn't start for close to a month, though we've had tryouts."

"It started out as such a good day..." Theo said wistfully before sighing, and it took all of my willpower not to scoop him up in my arms and pack him in bubble wrap to try to protect him.

Even as the professor started talking in the front of the small lecture hall, where I would have preferred to have been seated, I continued to whisper at Theo. "It still can be. Have you gotten a chance to explore campus yet? Been to The Big Dough?"

"What's that?" he asked, wide-eyed, and I grinned at his interest.

"The best campus bakery ever. They've got donuts as big as your hands. And the coffee is pretty good, too, from what I understand."

"Not a coffee drinker?"

"Nah. I'm high-energy enough on my own without needing extra caffeine. Besides, the stuff always tasted nasty to me." Flicking my eyes towards the front again, I resisted the urge to get up, to bring my micro recorder down closer. I didn't really need the audio component of the class, but it didn't hurt.

Theo, meanwhile, had pulled out the most ragged copy of our Spanish book that I'd ever seen, pages frayed, and once he opened it, covered in several different colors of highlights. I stared momentarily, which drew his attention, and he admitted, "I don't get this stuff. I've tried," he waved a hand to indicate the battered text, "but it goes right over my head."

"I can maybe help with that," I offered. "Maybe after I give you the grand campus tour? If nothing else, I can show you my technique."

His voice was so quiet, I almost didn't hear him. But I did, and I almost wish I hadn't. "As long as it isn't your technique to try and get down my pants."

"Ouch."

"Sorry," Theo whispered, and this time, his hand came to rest on my knee. "I shouldn't be making assumptions. Those guys just got in my head. And they're your teammates?"

More like my family, I thought, but I didn't want to admit that to Theo. How could I explain to him that, through the years, lacrosse had been the closest thing to family I'd ever known? That the camaraderie and brotherhood made me feel like I actually belonged somewhere? Ten minutes ago I might have confessed it to him, but now he had me wary as well.

In my silence, Theo had removed his hand, and put his hands back onto his desk, turning his attention to our professor and not so much tuning me out as actually focusing on class. I sighed a little bit, frustrated by the situation, but determined to pick up the conversation at the conclusion of class.

I took a few notes over the course of the class, mostly noting the different tenses the professor wanted us to use or made examples of, but otherwise, I spent a lot of the time observing the rest of the room. Aaron, with his frosh flunkies, was on the opposite side, looking like he was somewhere between taking a nap or just resting against his backpack. Most of my other classmates were diligently taking notes. Theo highlighted like crazy, pen flying on his notepad, making quick strokes of notes that I hoped made sense to him, because I couldn't understand what I read, even seated so close.

When class finally ended, I turned to face him, finding him averting his eyes from me. Sighing a bit, I reached out and poked him in the ribs, startling him enough that he looked up. "Come explore with me," I encouraged. "I'll even buy you the donut of your choice."

It took Theo a moment to respond, but when he did, it made me laugh. "Do they have Boston Creme?" When I nodded, a slow smile curled over his lips. "Okay. Should we drop our bags off first?"

"We can do that," I agreed, finally rising to stand and waiting for him to do the same. A quick scan of the room revealed that most of the class had already left — including Aaron. With that thought in mind, I tilted my head slightly, indicating that he should follow me, and out we went, heading towards the Nicholas P. Knobloch dormitory — better known as "The Nic." I scanned us in and we climbed the stairs to my third floor room that I shared with Brent.

Brent didn't even turn away from his game when I entered the room, and I just tossed my bag near my desk before turning back out again. I didn't know which frosh dorm Theo lived in, so I gestured to him to lead on and soon found myself being let into Tucker Hall. His roommate was definitely more...aware...of my presence than Brent had been of Theo's.

"Hey, Theo. Oh. Hey, Owen." His eyes went as wide as saucers as he spoke, almost as if he'd spoken out of turn, and he moved to make a quick exit. "Shit. Gotta use the bathroom. If you'll excuse me."

"No need to run, Harv," Theo assured his roommate. "We're just dropping this off"—he indicated his backpack, which he put near his desk —"and then heading off. Catch you later?"

"Yeah, sure." Even I could read the curious eyes, and I bet that Theo would be getting the third degree from his roommate later. My pulse quickened. Had they been talking about me?

I waited until we were outside of the room before I casually asked Theo, "He knows my name?"

Theo had the decency to blush. "He might have helped me look you up on the lacrosse team page after you helped me that day."

I smiled down at him. "Oh? Was I that interesting?"

"I thought so." Theo mumbled a bit, but I still understood him. He glanced up at me before looking back down again, guiding us through the hallways until we'd exited the dorm and were back out in the chilly January air. "Your lead, sir."

"I'm no sir," I countered. Still, I gave him the campus tour, operating under the assumption he could only place where the other dorms and lecture halls were. Our first stop was the library, where I explained, "Your student ID lets you do pretty much anything in there. Use a laptop, if you don't have one of your own, take out books, or go old school and use the microfiche machine. It's a pretty robust library, all in all."

"Cool."

"Yeah." We walked a bit further until we came across a newer building, one that was accessible right out of the box. "This is the Student Union building. The cafeteria is located here, but there's also a sandwich shop, workout facilities, and gathering spots for the school's clubs and organizations."

"This is pretty much the only place I've been besides the cafe and the lecture halls, for Pride

Council gatherings."

"You went to a Pride Council gathering and I missed it? Figures."

His head snapped up so quickly it was surprising he didn't give himself whiplash. "You're part of Pride Council?"

"I am. I have been since *my* frosh year. Haven't dated anybody in awhile though."

"Oh," was all Theo had to say for himself, and I had to wonder what he thought. Those pretty blue eyes were all introspective, and it had me curious if he was into me, too. My carnal nature would have loved to pin him against a wall and make him plead for mercy, but my more romantic side wanted the opportunity to get to know him, to find out what made him tick, to see if he'd even consider dating a big Black man from Kentucky.

We continued on our journey, with me pointing out more buildings and even the athletic fields before we reached our final destination: The Big Dough. "I saved the best for last."

"How did I not notice this place when I was in the bookstore?" Theo wondered aloud and I chuckled softly. "I mean, it's right next door!"

"I'm surprised your nose didn't lead you in, but you *were* preoccupied with your books, so. C'mon though, let's go in, treat's on me."

I always kept cash on hand from my paycheck. Not much, but enough so that I could do things like this, not that I ever did. I was happy to see Dash working the counter, and he greeted me heartily. "Owen, my brother, how are you today?"

"Glad it's Friday, Dash. How are you? Have you met Theo yet?" I nudged him to get his attention;

he'd been focusing on the donuts that, as I told him, were as big as his hands.

"No, I haven't had the pleasure. Theo, you look like you want one of those Boston Cremes. Am I close?"

Theo's face flamed a pretty shade of red. "Yeah, apparently I'm transparent today."

Dash's eyes crinkled. "Nah, I'm just that good. Anything to drink?"

"Medium coffee, two creams, one sugar."

"Coming right up." Dash went to work on the coffee, while I moved us further down the line, towards where we'd pay. Theo was still a bit fixated on his donut, and I grabbed his hand to tug him closer to me.

I hadn't intended to keep my hand in his for long, but his hand closed around mine, even as he offered me a shy smile. My heart raced at the feel of his hand in mine; it felt so small, yet so right. "I'm going to need that hand to pay," I warned him affectionately, and that was when Dash interceded.

"Nah, on the house today." I gave Dash a reproachful look. His financial situation was better than mine, but that didn't mean he could afford to be giving away free food and drinks. "Even your muffin and juice, Owen."

"Dash," I said warningly, but he silenced me with a dismissive hand.

"Let me do this for my friend on his first date." He gave me a wink, and this time it was my turn to feel my face flush. I hadn't thought of this as a date, but maybe it had kinda sorta turned out to be one? While I turned contemplative, Dash handed the donut and coffee to Theo, and a moment later, my blueberry muffin and orange juice were extended my way. "Go. Have fun. And tell me all about it later." He laughed and his eyes crinkled again; I couldn't help but smile back at him.

I led Theo off to a small booth, letting us settle in almost side by side as he started to scarf down his donut and I unwrapped my muffin. I wasn't that hungry, and I didn't really need the extra sugar, but one "bad" meal wouldn't kill me. "That good?"

"Delicious," Theo swore between bites, and I had to laugh at him. He'd even stolen his hand back so he was practically double fisting the donut. "I can't come here too often, though, or I'll be gaining my frosh fifteen in no time!"

"I did offer you the opportunity to work out with me," I reminded him.

"Yeah, and those teammates of yours," he countered darkly, and I closed my eyes momentarily as I sighed. I liked Theo; he was cute. But it was going to cause problems if he kept taking affront to anything and everything my teammates did — even when they were out-of-line like Aaron had been.

"You said it had been a good day up to that point though, right? So it was just Aaron? And his tagalongs?"

"Yeah."

"Look, I'm sorry for what they said, and for them even bothering you to begin with. I don't know what Aaron's problem is, beyond that he's a Callahan and thinks he owns this place." Theo looked confused, so I elaborated. "He's the third-generation to come to this school. He's a snob, and a bit of a know-it-all, but he's very good at face-offs, so we generally tolerate him. I swear to you the rest of the team isn't like him."

"How do I know that though?"

"Am I like that?" I asked him, staring into blue eyes that tried to blink and look away. "Am I?"

"Not in my experience, but I barely know you, Owen. I'd like to get to know you better, maybe even have Dash's comment about a first date be true, but everything I know about you so far is from the lacrosse page and what you told me in the bookstore. And everything you know about me is what you read on that class listing, and what Aaron spewed during class."

"How do you know I didn't try to stalk you?" I asked, and he raised an eyebrow at me. "I tried, but you had your page locked down." He nodded. "But I think at the very least we could connect on FisherFriends. And talk more." I paused briefly before remembering how the previous conversation about this topic had gone before plowing ahead. "And I can still show you my technique for Spanish. I think it might help you."

"I'll think about it," he murmured, looking down and away from me again and grabbing a napkin to clean off his fingers. I'd barely made a dent in my muffin, and he'd already demolished his donut. "It's not that I don't want to get to know you; I'm just scared, okay? If you'd asked me before this class I would have been all 'hell yeah,' but Aaron touched on all my deepest fears about coming here."

I reached across the booth to hook my fingers under Theo's chin, forcing his face upward until he looked at me. "We'll get that taken care of," I assured him. "And I'll show you I'm a good guy, worth your time and trust."

"I think I should head back to my dorm now," Theo answered softly. "I've got a lot of studying to do this weekend." It was a cop out, but I let him get away with it. I let his face go and finished off my orange juice in one gulp before moving to stand.

"C'mon. I'll walk you back, then." Despite his words, Theo rose almost reluctantly to his feet, swiping his hands on his jeans before falling in step beside me. I waved at Dash on our way out, signaling to him that I'd talk to him on FisherFriends later, before we exited.

The way back to Tucker Hall wasn't that long, and once we reached the door, Theo went to hurry inside. But before he could get too far, I hooked a hand around his elbow and turned him back towards me. This time, he held my gaze, and when I leaned closer, he sucked in a breath. He wasn't ready to kiss me yet — and I wasn't ready yet either, if I was being honest with myself — so I planted a soft kiss against his forehead and then let him go.

I turned to walk back to my own dorm when his voice called out, "Owen!" Looking back over my shoulder, I found that he'd followed me. "Could I have your cell phone number?" The voice was soft and shy but had a trace of determination in it.

Nodding, I rattled off the number to him, and with a finger wave, made my exit. I was grateful that Brent didn't have any evening classes tonight so that he could help me dissect this situation once I reached our room. It didn't take long to reach The Nic, or to climb those three flights to get to our shared space, and this time when I walked in, Brent turned to face me. "Who was he?"

"That was Theo," I responded, entering the room fully and moving to settle on my bottom bunk to relax.

Brent was aware I was pansexual, so I wasn't too horribly surprised when he asked, "So, is he a potential boyfriend? Or just a friend?"

"If I knew the answer to that." I sighed. "I like him, that's my overprotective streak, I think, but he's skittish as all hell. He's trans, and fucking Callahan was giving him the business, calling him a girl and harassing him about how he didn't belong at a school like RU."

"Fucking Callahan."

"Seems we say that a lot, don't we?" I snorted and shook my head. "But I gave Theo a tour of campus and finished off at The Big Dough. Dash Aziz from Pride Council was working and decided to comp our stuff. Which my wallet surely appreciated, but I dunno, I felt guilty about."

"Maybe because you never really had a bank account?" Brent countered. "I'd worry about you if you became an entitled son of a bitch like Callahan and expected free stuff from your friends and teammates when around campus." That would never happen.

"Never," I promised him. "And if I do, you have my permission to kick my ass."

"Like I could," he huffed, and we both laughed.

"You and several teammates?"

"More like it," Brent reasoned. "But tell me more about this Theo. Where's he from, what's he like, does he have a major?"

I shook my head. "I don't know. And I don't know what that means when it comes to my interest in him. Maybe it's too much based on trying to protect him and not enough on him as an actual person? Though I can change that, in time, if he'll let me. He did ask for my phone number before I left, so I can hope I'll get a text at some point."

"That would be good."

"Don't I know it," I agreed. "But the ball is on his side of the field. And I can't cross the mid-point line."

"Always with the lacrosse analogies."

I flipped Brent off, to his peals of laughter. When Brent turned back to his video game, I curled up properly on my bed, thoughts drifting. Theo didn't even really know me, beyond whatever he'd been able to find online. Would he like me once I told him how I'd grown up, with no real home, bouncing from house to house like a discarded children's playtoy? The muffin I'd had wasn't sitting so pretty in my stomach anymore.

Hazarding one last glance at my TracFone, which didn't have any new messages, I curled up tighter and closed my eyes. What a mess I'd gotten myself into this time.

5
Theo

It had been basically a week since I'd seen Owen last, since he'd kissed me on the forehead and sent my world spinning off its axis. Though I'd managed to ask for his number, I'd done nothing more than load it into my cell phone, having not found the courage to even text him with a simple "hello."

I had Intensive Spanish II next, and I was hesitating on even going to the class, worried about what I'd encounter from the lacrosse entourage. Ten minutes before class was to begin, I'd still not left, and Harv stared at me from across our room. "Do you want me to come with you?"

"Come with me?"

"Yeah," he started. "I could escort you there, and if needed, sit with you until the professor shows up. I know I'm no Owen, but I'd be willing to scare off the assholes if needed."

I gave Harv a shaky smile. "I appreciate that, I do, but I'm not sure it's necessary. I think I just need to get off my ass and head to class, be brave, and trust that they've gotten the message to leave me alone."

"That's all well and good, but what if they haven't? And since you've blown off Owen for the last week, there's no telling how he'd respond if they do start in on you."

"You're not helping," I growled, even as I rose to my feet and grabbed for my bag. "I'm going, okay? It'll be fine." Somehow having managed to convince Harv not to follow me, I left our room by myself.

Despite my words, I shivered a bit by the time I reached the lecture hall, peeking inside the classroom to see if I'd find what I suspected, and I did — Aaron, in his seat. I gave serious thought to waiting outside the classroom until the professor showed up.

But maybe I wasn't as smart as I thought I was, and with five minutes to spare before the professor was due, I walked into the classroom, heading straight for the back corner I'd occupied previously. Almost immediately footsteps trailed behind me, and as I settled in, I looked up to see Aaron with a demonic grin on his face. "Heeeeey, girl. What'd you do to your hair?"

I furrowed my brow, trying to figure out what he meant with his valley girl accent and also looking around him to see if Owen was in the room and able to assist. I thought I noticed him in the middle of the classroom, but before I could say or do anything, Aaron drew in closer, getting further in my face.

"I asked you a question, *girl*. You'd be wise to answer a *man* when he addresses you. Know your place."

So he wasn't just an idiot, he was a sexist idiot. Great. I couldn't figure out if I should answer him and oblige him, or ignore him and risk riling him up further. Where was the professor?

Before I could contemplate further, my redemption swooped in, in the form of Owen, whose voice trickled in ominously over Aaron's shoulder. "Is there a problem here?"

"The *girl* doesn't know her place," Aaron spat.

"Oh fuck off, Aaron. He's not a girl. Get over yourself, already." The two men looked like they were going to square off and fight, but the professor chose that moment to enter the classroom, and only after Aaron stalked off did Owen move to head back to his seat.

I managed to exhale once the class started properly and just focused on the professor, frantically taking notes and highlighting my book as we went along. This class couldn't end soon enough so I could get back to my dorm room and unwind. But my intentions, while good, were ill-planned. While Aaron may have considered coming back to harass me again on class completion, Owen got to me first, stopping me before I could get midway through the room.

"You've been avoiding me." There was no accusation in his tone, just a statement, if perhaps a bit of a question. Like he was trying to figure out why. I thought about telling him he'd rattled me so much, I'd needed some time to think things through.

"I was," I admitted, and though I ached to turn away and bolt for the door, my feet remained locked in their position, trapping me in conversation with him.

"Why?" The question was simple in its directness.

"Can we talk about this elsewhere?" I could feel eyes watching us, probably Aaron, and it was unnerving me.

Nodding tightly, Owen grabbed his bag, stopping only long enough to pick up a micro recorder from the professor's lectern before indicating I should follow. I hesitated for only a split second before following, letting him lead, quickly realizing we were heading back to his dormitory. That made me more nervous than I cared to admit, but I wasn't going to let him call me out on that if I could help it.

Once we'd labored up the steps and were in his room, I watched Owen walk to where his roommate sat in a beanbag chair, playing video games on their TV. Owen picked up a wireless set of headphones and handed them to the roommate, and after a brief but hushed conversation, the roommate was "plugged in" and the room was otherwise silent.

"Why?" he asked again, as I stood awkwardly at the end of his bed, rocking back and forth on my feet slightly.

"Because I didn't know what to think. I mean there was this initial, physical, attraction that I expected nothing more of. You were out of my league, and besides that, you were logically going to be straight. And then suddenly, you were there and there was mutual interest and I didn't know what to do with myself."

Owen tilted his head in a thoughtful manner. "I can understand that. Especially the expectation that you stand no chance with someone and then suddenly, there's a chance. So where do we go from here?"

"I'm not sure." I gulped. "I still think you're out of my league. I mean, you're big, strong, and attractive, and I'm tiny and..."

"Don't even say it."

"Say what?" I asked.

"Don't even dare imply that you're not attractive. Because you are. You've got the most amazing blue eyes I've ever seen. A smile, that while currently rare, lights up a room." Owen had folded his arms across his broad chest and stared at me, and all I could do was gulp again.

"Okay. Ignoring all of that momentarily," I started, but he growled. "Momentarily!" He waved me on, so I continued. "I like you. I'd even dare say I'm attracted to you. But I'm scared. I haven't really had good dating experiences, just people trying to take advantage of me."

Owen's face softened, and I swore a look of understanding passed through those brown eyes. "I like you too," was all he initially said, but at my waffling, he continued. "I'd like to date you, to prove to you that I am one of the good guys out there, that I'm not going to hurt you. Are you willing to give me that chance?"

Rather than immediately answer, I moved to sit on the edge of Owen's bed. To my surprise, he joined me, grabbing my hand and lacing our fingers together. When he gave my hand a slight squeeze, my voice quivered, but I answered. "I'm willing."

He smiled, and though it was wider than I'd ever seen previously, it still didn't quite reach his eyes. "You really are attractive to me, you know. I'd like nothing more than to sit here and kiss you breathless, kiss you until you believe that with every fiber of your being, know it to be the truth."

I couldn't help but shiver, and though I pulled my hand away from Owen's, it was only to shrug out of my backpack, which I shoved to the corner of his bed. Turning back to face him, I stared up into his eyes, wondering how long this blast of courage would last. I saw the surprise register in his eyes as I moved to lean in, to press my lips against his, and the hand that had been holding mine came up to cradle my jaw, a big thumb sliding along my skin.

My eyes fluttered shut and I started to tremble, already overwhelmed by the stark simplicity yet powerfulness of his actions. I don't think he was expecting my tongue to trace against his lips, but his mouth opened and our tongues came together, meandering about and getting to know each other, all the while sending my heart beating madly against my chest.

This man. Yes, I still barely knew him, but I wanted to know him intimately, to know every inch of his skin, and if his eyes went to slits when he was pleased, and if his skin took on a light sheen of sweat when he was aroused. It was too early for all of that, but that didn't stop the desire on my part. I inched closer to him, moving to thread a hand in his hair, to hold him to the kiss, and I could hear him rumble out a noise that could have been either a moan or a groan.

We kissed until my lungs burned, and only then did I pull back, panting for breath, locking eyes with Owen and seeing the hunger still present in him. "You," he took a deep breath, seemingly searching for words before settling on, "are very kissable." But even with his words, he pulled back slightly, seemed to rein himself in, even as his hand kept stroking along my face. "I want more than just physical though. I want to know you, Theo. What makes you smile, what makes you laugh. What keeps you up at night."

I shifted until my forehead leaned against his, and though I closed my eyes, a soft laugh filtered out. "Lately, you've been keeping me up at night. Wondering about you, why your team seems so important to you, what makes you tick. Wondering if two years seems as insurmountable to you as it does to me." Because how could it not? If this thing lasted more than a blink, he'd be graduated by *my* junior year, and then what?

"Two years is nothing, Theo."

"You could be anywhere in the country at that point, depending on where your future jobs take you. And then what?" I fretted, even though a part of me argued that logistically, I was worrying about the future way, way, *way* too soon.

A thumb gently caressed my cheek. "We'll worry about that when we get there. Or get closer to there. Let's leave our worries to right now, okay? That we can at least do something about."

"You're right, I know you're right," I conceded. "I just..."

"I understand," Owen whispered before his lips barely brushed against mine. It was just a fleeting kiss, lacking the heat of our earlier kisses, but it still made me shiver.

Drawing my eyes back open again, I found dark brown orbs locked on me. My lips curled into a smile, and I told him softly, "You make me smile, y'know. The way you've looked out for me, right from the start. Maybe I should feel offended that you feel like I need looking after, but you've got me feeling like I'm special. Precious even. I've never felt like that before."

"Good. I'm glad you feel that way." He paused for a moment, seemingly searching for words before telling me, "I haven't had the easiest of lives, so far. But Roseden has given me something I've never really had before — a family. The team, by and large, are my brothers-in-arms, who've got my back whenever I need them."

"Where does Aaron fit into that?" I wondered.

"I don't know," Owen answered, and I could tell he was being honest by the hoarse quality his voice took. "I've never particularly been a fan of the little cuss, because he's been handed everything all his life, but..."

"Your brain and your heart don't know how to agree on how best to deal with him?" I suggested, and he barely moved his head, just enough to nod.

"I need to call Coach, to make him aware of what Aaron is doing. Hell, we should probably go to the dean's office to make them aware of the harassment. Which means my brain acknowledges there's a problem here, a big one. But my heart still says, 'He's your teammate, you can fix this without getting the big guns involved.'" He sighed, briefly looking away from me.

Gently, I moved his chin until he was looking at me again, and this time it was my turn to press my lips against his. "I don't want to cause any trouble," I whispered to him. "Maybe I shouldn't have come here in the first place. It's not like my entire family wasn't aware something like this could happen. Not with that damn TV show in my history."

"Tell me about the TV show," Owen persuaded me, and though I sighed, I complied.

"Understand first that I was about seven when I told my parents I wasn't a girl anymore, I was a boy. They were shocked, understandably, but my dad particularly is the rational sort, and he took the news as something that needed to be studied and problem-solved. Not that I was a problem, but getting me in the right clothes, the right body, the right everything? *That* was a problem."

"So you were pretty young."

"I guess some kids are even younger when they realize. Maybe subconsciously I did, too. I hated everything about being a girl, from clothes to toys. Some would have called me a tomboy, but for me, it was much, *much* more. I'm pretty sure my mom still hides the scissors so I can't give myself haircuts. And I used to give myself such awful rashes, because even my skin didn't feel like it belonged on my body. The TV show, though? That came about when I was twelve. My parents thought it would be a good experience for me, and that the financials just made it a bonus. And while they were right about the money being helpful, the experience wasn't worth it."

"What makes you say that?"

"I started out my first year of high school in person, but the bullying forced me to switch to online classes by the second half of the year. There were a few guys who'd try and hook up with me, but I came to realize it was all a sick joke to them. Football players mostly, wanting to say they'd banged the guy with the pussy."

"That's a rather crude description," Owen cringed.

I shrugged. "It was what they said. So I have a healthy mistrust of my own gender now. Any guy who wants to get down my pants is going to have to prove they deserve to be there."

"Noted."

I cracked a small smile. "That wasn't directed at you, but that's okay. I don't expect it to happen any time soon." I waited half a beat. "Why do your smiles never seem to reach your eyes?"

"They don't?" I shook my head. "Well, like I said, my life to this point hasn't been the easiest. I'm a product of the State of Kentucky foster care system. My earliest memory is of my caseworker helping me carry a plastic bag filled with all my worldly goods. I apparently lived with my grandma at some point, but I have no memory of her or that time. So Amanda, my caseworker, was about the only consistency I had, beyond plastic bags of clothes every year or two, sometimes even less."

"So you don't know your parents?" I questioned sympathetically. "How did you end up at an expensive school like Roseden, given your situation?"

"Negative on the parentals. They gave me up when I was a baby, whoever they were. I'm guessing the situation at my grandma's wasn't that great for me not to remember it. But as for how I ended up here? I was in the top one percent of my graduating class in high school, so I had great grades, and I wanted a school that not only had a great History program of study, but some history itself. Roseden fit the bill. I'm on a full academic scholarship, but as you've seen, I work at the bookstore to supplement my income. It's how I can afford to have a cell phone, simple as it is."

My head was spinning again, mostly trying to imagine the life that Owen had described. How would I have ever gotten through a transition without the love and support of my family? No wonder Owen had such strong feelings about his team, though — if they really were a brotherhood, that would have filled a big hole in his life.

"Don't look so glum, chum. I'd like to think, despite it all, I'm a pretty happy, easy-going guy. I keep myself active, I play my favorite sport at the college level, and I've got a good group of friends in the Pride Council. There's no pity needed here."

Without even a thought, I leaned closer to kiss Owen again, this time with a bit of heat to it. Our tongues tangled and fought for possession of our mouths, caressing and carousing paths perhaps not presented previously. I could feel a moan building in my throat, feel my pulse quickening, but it wasn't until Owen's hand slipped back behind my neck and held me to the kiss that the heady noise left my body.

Again and again our tongues intertwined until it was impossible to tell where one ended and the other began. He was intoxicating, getting me more drunk than any illicit glass of wine I'd ever snuck had remotely done. I whimpered when he pulled away and used a hand to cling to him, to try and keep him close. He did break the kiss though, leaving us both panting with need and desire. The door snicked shut, and I guessed that Brent had noticed our activities and decided to take his leave.

"No pity." I gasped out a breath. "Got it."

Owen dragged fingertips along the back of my neck, making me shiver with want, but he left his teasing at that and removed his hand, shifting it back to the front of my head, beginning to caress my cheek once more. "I'm guessing the surgery you had this fall was top surgery?" I nodded, though I lowered my head, slightly embarrassed. "As young as you were, did you have much for them to do? I imagine you were on puberty blockers, right?"

"I was," I whispered. And then, doing something I never did, I offered shyly, "I can show you the scars if you want."

"An opportunity to see you shirtless?" a husky voice breathed near my ear. "Yes please!"

Though I shivered, I pulled back and away from Owen until I had actually climbed off the bed. Grabbing my backpack, I moved to discard it next to his, and only then did I start the process of stripping out of my parka, sweater, and T-shirt, slowly revealing the pale skin beneath.

When all was said and done, a dark hand stretched out to trace lightly along the crescent shaped scars beneath where my breasts had once sat. It was like Owen was mapping out my body, taking in the scars and incorporating that into his mental catalog of what made me, me. Despite him lavishing attention on me, I didn't like being exposed and reached for my T-shirt, tugging it back into place.

Seeming to sense my unease, Owen pulled away from me and resettled further up the bed, losing his parka along the way. Holding his arms open, his eyes silently beckoning me closer, I eventually ended up curled against his chest, sighing happily when my cheek ended up over his heart. "This is good," I whispered.

A big hand moved and ended up behind my head, just holding me in place as fingers lightly slid through my hair. I was pretty sure if he kept touching me like that, that I could fall asleep, but I didn't say that to him. I think he understood, even without words. "I've got you."

Owen

There was something incredibly endearing about Theo being so comfortable with me that he could curl up on my chest and be content. The arm loosely hooked around my neck just furthered the "awww" factor, and I was a very lucky young man to have him so close to me. When I leaned closer to kiss his forehead, he glanced up at me, blue eyes bright and happy.

I smiled. "What?" he questioned.

"Just you," I told him. "You're so adorable all curled up so close. I just want to snuggle you forever."

I laughed when he wrinkled his nose. "I'm not adorable." When I laughed harder, he huffed. "I'm not!"

"You are," I informed him, barely brushing my lips against his. "You so are."

He tried to keep his face disgruntled, but there was a smile tugging at the edges of his lips, and I grinned quietly to myself. This sweetie was mine to treasure and worship and love on, and I intended to keep him around for a long while. "Owen?" he questioned with a tinge of sleepiness in his voice. "How did you learn how to play lacrosse?"

"Police athletic leagues when I was growing up. My foster parents would dump me off there and I learned a variety of sports. I'm not a half bad baseball player, but I loved the speed, the adrenaline rush, of lacrosse. The only thing I've heard can compare is hockey. But at least when I was little, I didn't have to worry about coming up with equipment or anything like that — they supplied it. And even though the high school team was pretty awful, at least we had one."

"I'm glad you had that," he murmured, and I quietly ran a hand through his hair. He was going to fall asleep soon, I could tell.

"I presume you chose Theo as your name? What made you pick it?"

"Is Grandpa," Theo mumbled into my chest. "Was named after him, Thea. He was super important in my life, so it felt like a way to continue to honor him. He's gone now, but when he was alive, I was his buddy. I'm sure, before my parents understood that transgender is nature and not nurture, that they thought Grandpa made me this way, but all he did was love me for who I am. Always."

I couldn't help the pang in my chest, the reaction to him having someone in his life that important. Maybe I would be at some point, but there were no guarantees. Confident as I always tried to pass myself off as, growing up the way I did left its mark. Theo shifted a bit on top of me, nuzzling his face against my neck, and I smiled again. He truly was going to be asleep in no time. I let several minutes of silence pass us by before I tried whispering, "Hey, Theo?"

I wasn't surprised when I received no reaction in return except him shifting a bit closer to me. So I continued to run a hand through his hair, keeping him comfortable and close. It still amazed me a bit that he wanted to be there, that despite the hell he'd been through, even here, that he was willing to show me that level of trust.

A sneaker squeaked and I realized that Brent must have come back in at some point. But now he'd gotten up again and made it about halfway to the door when he realized that my eyes were open and he made a sign with his hands for "sleep" while pointing at Theo. I nodded and he nodded back, before he pointed towards the door and flashed me five digits. So he'd be right back and was probably running to the bathroom.

I focused on Theo in his absence, the little noises he made in his sleep, the way that when he was at peace, a small smile tugged at his lips. I wondered briefly if I was ever *that* calm, to smile in my sleep. I doubted it sincerely. I'd been woken up in the middle of the night too many times to collect all of my stuff to think that sleep was a safe place. I was glad it was for Theo, though.

When Brent came back in, he moved to settle in my desk chair instead of his beanbag chair. "All good here?" he asked under his breath, gesturing to Theo and I.

I glanced down at Theo and then up at Brent. "I think so. He's giving me the opportunity to be his boyfriend, so there's that."

Brent's grin could have lit up the room. "Good. I'm glad. You were moping this last week and that wasn't a pretty look on you."

"Shut up," I huffed, as quietly as I could muster. "You know you always think I'm pretty."

He batted his eyelashes at me but the grin remained. "Always," he swore, crossing his heart with his hands.

It took me biting hard on my lip not to burst out in laughter, and I could see Brent was having the same problem with how much his eyes danced. I let the silence reign supreme before I got serious, turning a bit more towards Brent and telling him softly, "Y'know, if anyone could make me believe in love, it might be this guy."

"I told you that you just needed to find the right person," he answered knowingly. "The cow was not the right person."

"Tell me about it," I moaned, then glanced at Theo to see if he stirred, even going so far as to poke him lightly in the ribs. No response. Letting out a sigh of relief, I turned my attention back to Brent. "Let's not talk about the cow anymore, yes?"

He gave me a thumbs up and then watched Theo for a moment. "I do like seeing this though. He's comfortable with you. It takes a lot of trust to fall asleep on someone."

"I'm just glad we're finally getting to know each other. I'll poke his birthday out of him soon enough, and any other dates he feels are important." I watched the rise and fall of Theo's chest before my eyes drifted back to Brent. "Do you think I should offer to escort him to classes? It seems like Spanish is the only class he's having issues with bullying, but..."

"I think it depends on how you present it. Are you being the dutiful boyfriend and walking him to class so you can sneak a kiss out of him before you go where you need to go? Or are you taking him solely because you're concerned for his safety?"

"Some combination of the two?" I retorted. "Can't there be a happy medium? I'd like to be with him because I genuinely enjoy his company and want to spend as much time with him as possible, but I also want to ensure his safety. I'm just not sure how he'd feel about that."

"So ask him once he wakes up again. At the rate we're going, that won't take long." I flipped him the bird. His voice went softer, even as he let out a low chuckle. "In all seriousness though, that really is a question for him and his independence. He could love you with all of his heart and still want to be able to walk to classes on his own to prove he can do it, y'know?"

"Yeah, I get you." I stroked a hand through Theo's hair, feeling him shift to push up against the touch slightly. Without letting my eyes drift away from Theo, I asked Brent quietly, "What am I going to do about Aaron?"

"Talk to Coach," he answered immediately. "And before you interrupt me, he's the adult in immediate supervision of us. If anyone can do anything, it's him. And I have faith he will."

I made a bit of a face. "And what if it's outside his jurisdiction? It's not a team matter, it's a school matter. We should probably be going to Theo's dean. I just..."

"You're worried about the effect ratting out your teammate will have on the rest of the team." I nodded, keeping my eyes on Theo the entire time to ensure he didn't wake. "It could cause trouble. I'm not sure if there's any way to avoid that. There'll be those who side with you, who'd do what you're thinking about doing. Then there'll be those who think it's just locker room banter and needs to be ignored."

"And you?"

"You have to ask?" Brent scoffed at me. "I've got your back, always. And I think Callahan is way out of line, and I don't even know what he did today, but I'm trusting he did *something* today."

"He did," I confirmed. "He was calling Theo a girl again, and telling him to know his place. If it was disturbing to me, I can only imagine how Theo felt."

"I wasn't really a fan," murmured a soft voice against my chest before he turned and faced Brent. Running a sleepy hand through his hair, he extended the other hand outward. "I don't think we've met properly. I know you're the roommate, and you probably know I'm the boyfriend. But I'm Theo."

"Brent." They shook hands before Theo pulled back and cuddled against me again. "Didn't mean to wake you up with our talking."

Theo yawned. "It was going to happen. I shouldn't be napping during the day; it disrupts my sleep at night. And I already have bad dreams about guys like Aaron playing boogeyman in the night."

I growled and Theo tilted his head up to kiss my nose. "Sorry, I don't like that he's gotten in your head that much. I want to shake him until I break him."

"We don't need you getting kicked out of school," Theo countered. "And besides, it was a faceless boogeyman to start. Remember, I came here with those worries."

"I know." I sighed. "I just want to wrap you in bubble wrap and protect you." Theo quirked a smile at me. "In that regard," I started, and he raised an eyebrow, "how would you feel about me walking you to classes, including Spanish?"

Theo tilted his head up so he was better able to look at me. "Is this cuz you're my boyfriend now and want to spend time with me? Or because you want to keep me safe? Either way, I'm good with it, so long as it's not disrupting your work, class, or lacrosse. Deal?"

"Deal," I agreed happily. "I'm a bit like a pit bull though; my bark is way worse than my bite. That's not to say I won't throw my weight around if necessary, but I try not to resort to that."

"That's true even on the field," Brent added. "Owen stands his ground, but he's not out there, flying around, trying to hit everything that moves. There's a time and a place for that kinda stuff."

Theo wrinkled his nose a little bit. "Let's not talk about violence, okay? Owen, didn't you have a Spanish technique you wanted to teach me?"

"Sure. Brent, could you hand me my laptop?" I shifted Theo around in my arms until his back was to the wall, he was on my right side, and I was able to balance the school's laptop on my lap.

"I'm going to get going to class. You two have a good afternoon." Brent rose, moving back to his desk to grab his backpack, snagging a tablet off his desk, and sliding it under his arm.

"Bye, Brent, nice meeting you." I bit my lip not to chuckle, because despite his words, Theo was totally focused on me and not my roommate.

"Nice finally meeting you too, Theo. He's been like a love-sick puppy waiting for you to give him a chance. Thanks for that." I had nothing close by to throw at Brent, and it didn't matter; he was out the door before I could have taken aim.

I muttered briefly and shifted a bit more on the bed, trying to get comfortable while waiting for the antiquated laptop to load up. "How old is this?"

"Dunno. It's the school's. They loan it to me. I could probably afford a cheap one of my own, but it's hard to justify spending that much money, plus paying for software. This one has everything I need. It's just...slow."

Theo's hand found one of mine and gave it a squeeze of reassurance, almost as though he was telling me he didn't care that I needed the school's help to do things most students came by naturally. "I'm glad you have it."

"Me too." I finally was at the desktop and I quickly loaded up Anki, explaining to Theo, "This is the main app I use for Spanish, and for a few other classes as well. But it's really useful for Spanish. It makes flash cards and uses spaced repetition, or srs. Ever heard of that?"

He shook his head. "I've used flashcards though; how is this different?"

"I'm glad you asked." I turned to kiss his temple before continuing. "So with spaced repetition, it works on the premise that the best time to learn something is right before you're about to forget it. So this shows you the flash cards just as you're about to forget the topic, word, or phrase."

"Ooooooh. That sounds interesting. Show me?"

"Part of the fun, or challenge, depending on how you look at it," I explained, "is that you create the cards yourself. So your very first commitment to memory is the card creation. Any audio you might add, like our professor speaking, or pictures to remind yourself of cues, that's all on you. That's why I record audio in class."

"An example?" he prompted, and I tickled him for being so impatient.

"I'm getting there!" Theo huffed between his giggles, but he still gestured for me to continue. "So like today, we were working on the simple past tense. If we used *tener*, the *yo* form would be *tuve*. Now there's several ways we could do that on a card, and we might just do all of them. We could create a card showing all the simple past tenses of *tener*, so we get exposed to all of them at once, and have to fill them in, so we memorize the format that *tener* uses, as an irregular verb. Another thing we could do is make a sentence that utilizes *tuve*. Like for you, you could say, '*Tuve una cirugía en el otoño.*' You had surgery in the autumn."

"Okay, that sorta makes sense. And you say this will next show me the card or cards when I'm in danger of forgetting this information?"

"Exactly," I confirmed with a happy smile. "And when you see it next depends on how well you think you responded to your exposure to it. If you got it easily, you can send it out for the longest time. If you struggled a bit, you can have it show sooner."

"This sounds like it could be a game-changer. Where did you learn this?"

"Middle school. I was always a good student, but sometimes, because of my situation, I struggled to retain information. A very kind teacher introduced me to spaced repetition and especially how well it works with languages, and I've been utilizing it since."

Theo cuddled closer to me. "I'm glad that teacher cared enough to show you that trick. And that you cared enough to show it to me. Maybe there's hope for me in Spanish yet."

"I'll do my level best to help you," I swore to him, and I got a light smile in return. "Let me put this laptop aside, and then we can go back to snuggling."

"I like that idea." He pulled just enough away from me that I could climb from the bed and return the laptop to the desk, making sure it was far enough away from the edge that it wouldn't fall. When I turned back to the bed, Theo was just lying there, an innocence to him, and it took my breath away. "What?"

"You. Just you," I whispered reverently and climbed back in, shifting around until he curled up against my chest again. "This is perfection."

"You are."

I barked a laugh. "Oh, babe, I'm so far from perfect. I've got plenty of flaws, some potentially fatal. But I do think the world of you and will do my best to take care of you."

"Babe. I like that." Theo's face took on a faint pink hue and I gave him a nose-to-nose kiss. "And I've got flaws too. Maybe what we are is perfect for each other?"

"I can agree with that." And then I teased, "So what you're telling me is I needed a pocket sized boyfriend that I could carry with me wherever I go?" I got whacked in the stomach for my troubles. "Hey!"

"I am not pocket sized," he hrmphed.

"You're the perfect size," I assured him. Theo's eyes brightened again, and I nudged him slightly until he was back properly curled up against my chest. "Rest. I can walk you back to your dorm later if you want, but in the meanwhile, take advantage of your Owen-pillow."

"My new favorite pillow."

I couldn't explain, to him or even myself, how much that warmed my heart to hear.

7

Theo

Days turned into weeks and we were now quickly approaching lacrosse season, which meant that Owen worked himself to the bone trying to stay in top physical shape. Despite that, our routine was pretty normal now, with Owen waiting for me outside of my dorm and then accompanying me to my classes before heading off his own way.

When he came to pick me up for today's Spanish lesson, though, I wasn't having any of it. "You're sick," I proclaimed. "Your face is flaming and you're burning up."

"It's just a little cold, I'll be fine," he protested, but I stood my ground and insisted on escorting him back to The Nic. "I'm really not that bad off," he tried again, even as he yawned dramatically.

"Just rest. Let me borrow your recorder, and I'll get us fresh audio for our Anki sessions."

"If Aaron gives you any trouble..." Owen warned, as we stood outside The Nic, his dorm mates walking around us to get inside.

"He won't," I assured him. "He'd be stupid to at this point. He's seen us walking in together, holding hands. He's got to realize that we're together."

Owen sighed but didn't argue and instead leaned closer to give me a kiss on the cheek. "I'll rest. I promise. But I am sending Brent to pick you up after class. He's got time; he can afford to do it."

I didn't even bother protesting; I just pointed towards the door, which Owen ultimately trudged through. My poor sweet teddy bear. I hoped he would feel better soon. But in the meanwhile, I needed to scurry off to class to both ensure I wouldn't be late and to set up Owen's recorder.

I barely beat the professor in the door, pausing only long enough to leave the recorder on his lectern before I took a seat in the middle of the classroom, notebook and text out to follow along with the instructor. But even from where I sat, I could feel eyes burning a hole through me, glaring at me, and I wasn't sure what I'd done to draw Aaron's ire this time, beyond simply existing.

Knowing and understanding Owen's study methods made paying attention in Spanish a whole lot easier than it had been. I still hadn't done that well on the first major quiz, mixing up my tenses, but that too would improve in time. Or so I kept telling myself. The stress of actually being at school — and having to deal with an asshole like Aaron — meant my grades were suffering as a whole.

When class ended, I packed up quickly, even remembering to grab Owen's recorder, before I booked it towards the door. But I wasn't quite fast enough, and Aaron intercepted me and drove me off towards the front corner of the room. "So I see you're making Owen sick," he started, and it was so different from his usual tactics, that it threw me off.

"I didn't make him sick," I ventured, but he tutted and interrupted me.

"Of course you did. Constantly running after you, babysitting you because you're too weak to protect yourself. You're an embarrassment." I could feel the heat rise to my face, because I'd be lying if I said that wasn't a concern I'd thought too, but I'd never dared voice it. "But I'm prepared to make a deal with you."

I looked at Aaron suspiciously. Any deal he wanted to make was liable to be bad for me. But yet I found myself wondering, curious, so I asked, "What?"

"Stay away from Owen." I almost managed to get out a noise of protest before he shushed me and continued. "And I'll leave you alone, and make sure the rest of my teammates do as well. None of them like you, you're a distraction, and it's only a matter of time before Owen hurts himself in the weight room or on the field with you messing around with him."

I gulped. I'd never met any other teammates besides Brent, and he seemed to like me just fine, but maybe that was because he was Owen's roommate? What if what Aaron said was true, and I was a distraction? Didn't I owe it to Owen to let him have a good lacrosse season, to continue to excel here at Roseden? Licking my lips, I whispered to Aaron, "Brent will be here soon. I need to give him Owen's recorder. Then I'll think about what you said."

Aaron gave me a short nod and then turned to exit, leaving me tucked in the corner of the classroom, trying to compose myself. My heart pounded, beating out of my chest. The last thing I wanted to do was cause Owen pain, but it seemed like I needed to do so in the short-term to rescue him long-term from the likes of me. Just about the time I gathered myself up, Brent poked his head into the room. "Hey you, you coming?"

I shook my head and gave him Owen's recorder. "Give that back to him, will you? I...need to go. I'm sorry." I scurried past him, even despite hearing him calling my name, but eventually his voice trailed off and I was able to make a brisk walk to Tucker Hall, where Harv was waiting for me.

"You look like you've seen a ghost," he noted. "What happened? Where's Owen?"

"I need to break up with him."

"*WHAT?*" Harv's voice was loud, so loud that he likely woke the neighbors if they were sleeping.

"Shush, quiet." Harv rolled his eyes, but gestured for me to continue on. "I'm a distraction to his academics and his athletics. He's sick because he's been constantly on the go, chasing after me, trying to protect me. If I was man enough, I wouldn't need protection."

Harv studied me thoughtfully, though he nudged me towards my desk chair while he went to sit in his. "Ignoring the Owen aspect of this momentarily, do you really feel like having him escort you makes you less of a man?"

I only hesitated a split-second before I nodded. "I know I'm slight, and someone with ill intentions could run roughshod over me. Hell, how do I even know that Owen's intentions are good?"

"If you really have to ask yourself that, maybe you shouldn't be in a relationship with him. But I don't think Owen is the problem here." He looked at me knowingly, as if he was reading my mind, and it creeped me out a bit. "Someone, likely Aaron, got in your head and preyed on your fears. So I'm going to sit here with you until we straighten this out."

"Your class," I protested, and he waved me off.

"Missing one class is not going to kill me. Besides, getting my friend back straightened out with his *boyfriend* is more important. You've been so happy these last few weeks. Don't let one asshole take it away from you."

I sighed and lowered my head so that Harv couldn't see my eyes. "He told me I made Owen sick, that I was a distraction to him and the rest of the team. That no one on the team liked me, and he'd save me further abuse if I left Owen alone."

"A devil's deal," Harv mused. "He wins regardless of your answer. You agree to back off, he's made you and Owen both miserable, which he clearly views as a viable option at this point. You disagree, and you've all but committed to having him harass you for the foreseeable future." He paused half a tick. "You really should talk to your dean about him. His actions are against the Code of Conduct."

Leaning back in the chair, I sighed. "I like Owen. A lot. A lot, a lot. But I don't want to mess him up, mess up his life after school. He's worked so hard to get where he is; he doesn't need some *girl* from New England messing with his flow."

"Do *not* let me ever hear you call yourself a girl again," Harv growled, and before I was fully aware of what was happening, he was in front of me, grabbing my jaw and forcing me to look up at him. "You are not a girl, you never were, and just because that prick has a hard-on for you doesn't mean you need to listen to him!"

I blinked. "Do you think that's his problem? He's attracted to me, but can't get past the fact that I'm male?"

He let go of my jaw and moved back to his chair. "I wouldn't be surprised. He's a homophobe of the worst kind. He can't just spew his kind of nonsense and be easily ignored, no. He's got to stomp his feet and twist his words and make sure he has your attention before he verbally vomits."

"So what do I do?"

"If I were you?" Harv questioned, and I nodded. "I'd text Owen, let him know you're on your way over, and can he let you in. And once he does, and you're in there, you tell him this whole sordid tale, including the fact that you thought walking away might be the answer."

"That'll upset him," I worried.

"As it should," he countered. "And in the meanwhile, I'm going to look into clubs and programs around here for self-defense. I can't make you six inches taller, but I can help you feel safer. And I'm sure if Owen knew you wanted to bulk up, he'd help you in the weight room. He's a good guy."

"You're right." I sighed, reaching into my pocket for my cell phone. I stared at it for a long moment before I unlocked the screen, finding a text waiting for me from Owen asking what had happened, and then another asking why I was ignoring him. Shaking my head slightly, I let my fingers zoom over the screen until I'd tapped out my message.

Me: I'm headed to The Nic right now. You up for letting me in?

The response started coming through within seconds.

Owen: I'll be down there waiting for you.

Looking up at Harv, I managed a sort-of smile. "There's still time for you to get to class, y'know. And thank you. I might have eventually come to this conclusion on my own, but it would have taken me a few days. And that wouldn't be fair to Owen."

"Or you." At my raised eyebrow, Harv snorted. "You're important too, lest you forget that. So it matters if the situation is fair to you."

Climbing to my feet, I crossed the room to pull my roommate into a hug, squeezing him extra tight before pulling back. "I've got to get going; I've got a boyfriend to straighten shit out with."

"I'd say good luck, but you won't need it. Everything will work out fine."

This time I quirked more of a smile. "Easy for you to say, but I think you might be right." Waving, I exited our room, heading towards the main door with the intention of making the trek to The Nic. The journey between dorms never took long, and before I even made it to the door of Owen's building, I could see his face peering through the glass, waiting for me.

When he opened the door, he tugged me into a hug, asking immediately, "What did that little asshole say to you?"

"We'll talk in your room," I returned, taking a deep breath but moving to thread my hand into his, needing his closeness, his comfort, as much as I needed to breathe.

That put a stumbler in Owen's step, but he led on until we were crossing through the familiar doorway. Once inside, he stripped me out of my parka and sweater before leading me to his bed, lying down and indicating that I should curl up on him, which I did. "Talk to me."

Sighing, I pressed my face against his chest, knowing my voice would be muffled, but also knowing that he would understand me. "He changed tact. He told me none of your teammates liked me, that I was a distraction to you, and I made you sick." He growled, but he didn't otherwise interrupt me. "He told me if I broke up with you, he'd stop bothering me and make sure none of your other teammates did either."

"And you actually considered that?"

"What if I am making you sick?" I countered. "You *are* running around between your job and working out and trailing after me because I'm too much of a wuss to stand up for myself."

"I'm not doing anything I don't want to be doing. I should get some say in this." Owen's voice was soft, almost dangerously so, but I thought his anger wasn't so much at me as it was at Aaron.

"He just...pushed all my buttons, hit upon almost all of my fears. I don't want to be dragging you down, Owen, not when you've got the world at your fingertips. You don't need me or anyone else holding you back."

"You don't hold me back; you make me feel alive." His voice strained, the emotion in it obvious, and I clung to him, guilt tearing me up from the inside. He took a deep, albeit shaky, breath and continued. "We need to work on your confidence, babe. I know we're relatively new, but he shouldn't have been able to sway you so easily."

"I'm sorry," I mumbled, and one of Owen's big hands slid through my hair. "I need to be stronger, braver. Harv said he'd look into self-defense classes for me, and suggested that maybe you could help me bulk up."

"We could do that. But if you're genuinely concerned about distracting me from my season, maybe we recruit another athlete in to help out. I think I know just the person, too."

I lifted my head off Owen's chest to gaze at him curiously, and he managed a smile at me before he pressed closer so our lips connected. It was easy to lose myself to him, to the kiss, to everything that he was, and everything we could be. When his tongue traced against my lips I eagerly granted him entrance and the heat level of the kiss increased exponentially.

My hand tightened in his T-shirt, threading into the material while his hand in my hair held me to the kiss. I could feel the heat coming off his forehead, but it still took me a moment to break the kiss, leaving me panting for breath.

"Who did you have in mind? Anyone I know?" I gazed into his eyes, seeing so much emotion reflected in them that it made my heart thud in my chest.

"A football player on Pride Council by the name of Ethan Kim. He's also student body vice president, so he might not have as much time as he'd like, but I bet he'd be willing to help or knows someone who can."

A low laugh slid from my lips, and at Owen's raised eyebrow, I explained, "I know Ethan; I met him and his boyfriend Joshua at Pride Council."

"I'll send him a direct message later and see what he has to say. But we'll get you feeling better about yourself. Because hearing that I almost lost you just about killed me. Please don't do that to me again."

I cuddled closer to him, shifting around until my face was against his neck, and pressed small kisses to his skin, quietly, reassuringly, trying to swear to him without words that I wouldn't hurt him if I could help it. His arms wrapped around my back, holding me close, and I just kept kissing him over and over again. He shivered, but this time it had nothing to do with his sickness.

Once more Owen's hand ended up threaded in my hair, fingers gliding slowly through strands in a soothing touch. I made a noise of contentment against his throat, and he made a happy sound in return.

"You need to rest," I whispered against his skin. "I'll stay close though."

"Please do," he answered. "'M sure I'll feel better when I wake up."

Nodding, I nuzzled him, periodically kissing his neck until his breathing evened out and he started to lightly snore. Even then I continued to kiss, wanting to comfort him, wanting to assure him I wouldn't leave.

Letting my hand shift until it settled over his heart, I swore I could hear it beating out a rhythm in words...

Stay close, stay close, stay close, stay close...

8

Owen

I wasn't sure how or when I fell asleep, but as I woke up, I became aware of the weight of another body on top of mine. It took me a moment to realize that Theo was curled on top of me, not quite asleep, but not really awake either. Lowering my mouth to gently kiss his forehead, I offered him a growly, sleep-tinged, "Hey."

He smiled up at me. "Hey yourself. Get some good rest?"

"I think so." My face no longer felt warm and I added, "I think my fever broke, and I'm feeling much better."

Theo grinned wider. "Best news I've heard all day. Does that mean I can kiss you silly again?"

I laughed softly, rubbing my cheek against the top of his head. "I'm already silly. And you never need an excuse to kiss me, babe. I can be breathless and blue from lack of oxygen, and I'll still want your kisses."

He went a delightful shade of pink but pressed closer to me, kissing along the curvature of my neck and nipping at my Adam's apple before letting his lips touch mine, the kiss, at first at least, gentle and unassuming. I relaxed into the touch even as I shifted to hold him closer, not wanting to ever let him escape my grasp.

As my hands moved along Theo's back and beneath his T-shirt he growled against my lips, kissing me harder while his tongue swept possessively through my mouth. It was ironic. There were those that would view him as the weaker of the two of us, but it was Theo who had me wrapped around his fingers, who could melt me with a simple kiss.

At the feel of my hands against his skin, he shivered but pressed closer, one of his hands sliding down to dip beneath my T-shirt. "Off," he whispered against my lips, and I moved quickly to oblige, dislodging him slightly in the process, but losing the shirt to the oblivion of the corner of my bed.

"Off," I repeated back at him, lightly tugging at his T-shirt but ultimately leaving it in his hands. He was still dealing with a lot of gender dysphoria and might not be comfortable being so exposed, even with me. But Theo sat up and yanked his T-shirt off, letting it join mine before he pressed our chests together, his skin all but scalding mine. "Goddddd." My voice was low and husky.

Theo kissed me, all over my face and against my lips, stealing my breath away while one of his hands lightly pawed at my skin. He had well-manicured nails — he was definitely going to leave his mark. "You make me want to question every ounce of sanity I have," he growled against my ear, and when I pulled back from him slightly to look at him curiously, he explained, "I want you, God I want you, but that wouldn't be good for either one of us right now. I'm not ready, and you shouldn't have to deal with the aftermath of that mistake."

Sucking in a deep breath but understanding immediately where he was coming from, I tugged him down so that we were chest to chest, skin to skin, and I rested my chin on the top of his hair. "So let's slow things down," I drawled softly. "Still touch, just not as frantic. I can wait for you, wait for us. Because when it does happen, I know it'll be amazing."

"Thank you." I brought a hand to his cheek, dragging my thumb along the planes of his face, feeling him shiver slightly as I did so. "You make me so happy, Owen."

"That's good." I nuzzled his hair. "Because you make me happy, too." Hazarding a glance across the room to our alarm clock, I groaned. "That being said, if you'd like to keep your virtue intact, Brent will be back shortly. We should probably throw shirts back on again."

Theo nodded his understanding and went fishing at the end of the bed for our shirts, first throwing me mine, and then tugging his over his head. A soft but sad sigh left his lips; he was going to miss the skin on skin contact as much as I was.

It couldn't have been five minutes after we'd gotten redressed that Brent returned, peeking into my bunk before fully entering. "Y'all are decent? Good."

"How'd you know I'd be here?" Theo wondered aloud.

Brent smirked at him. "Because I'm smart like that. It would take a stupid man to miss how crazy you two are about each other. A little hiccup wasn't going to change that. I knew once you got your head on straight, you'd be back."

Theo rolled slightly until he was able to grab an eraser off my desk, which he promptly threw in Brent's direction. My roommate easily dodged the projectile and laughed in Theo's direction. "Damn athletes," Theo muttered, even as he snuggled closer to me.

"Yeah, we're so horrible, ain't we?" I teased, nuzzling and kissing the top of his head.

"I can hardly stand being in the same room as you two," he deadpanned, and we all cracked up.

"I know, the muscles blind you, don't they?" I flexed to emphasize my point, and Theo faked a swoon in retort.

"They're so…hard," he answered with a filthy little grin curving over his lips.

"Eeeehhhhhssshhh no. I don't want to hear about hard things on my roommate, thank you very much!" Scooping the eraser off the floor, Brent chucked it back in our direction; I swatted it away without much effort. With Theo pressing his face against my neck to try and smother his giggles, I was happier than I could remember in a long time.

But the moment didn't last; Theo soon rose off me and moved to climb from the bed. I gazed at him curiously and he gave me a sad smile. "I need to head back and study. You need some more rest. And Brent would probably like to be able to go change into stuff to workout in without an extra set of prying eyes."

"As long as you don't leer at me like he does," Brent chirped, and I flung the eraser back across the room, pelting him in the side, to which he made a noise of protest.

"That's it, I'm telling Misha that you've been flirting with me again. Maybe she'll punish you." His girlfriend attended our sister school, nearby Cordelia Russell College, an all-women's academy. Brent had come back from one of their "dates" with handcuff marks on his wrists, and I'd never stopped letting him hear the end of it.

Theo waved his hand in front of his face, blushing and still giggling. "You two are like comedy gold. If I don't get out of here soon, someone'll have to pick me up off the floor because I'll be rolling around on it, laughing." Despite his words, I watched him pluck his sweater from where it landed, tugging it on.

"You really are going," I noted with a sigh, and he nodded at me. "Alright. I guess I can get more rest. I probably need it, even though I don't feel sick anymore."

"Do you want me to play doctor with him, Theo?" Brent wiggled his eyebrows, but he was working towards a degree in Sports Medicine and really did make a good nursemaid.

"No." Theo ran a hand across my face with affection, dragging his thumb over my lips. When he did so I kissed it gently, earning me an easy smile. "No one else touches my teddy bear except me." "Teddy Bear" I mouthed at him, and he nodded. "I'd just call you a bear, but you're not that hairy. So you're a teddy bear."

I shook my head, but I was smiling. "Shoo then, you. Pull on that parka and scoot back to Tucker Hall, and get cracking on those books. And if you decide you need or want a study buddy, I'm only a text away."

Grabbing his parka, Theo zipped himself up and then leaned closer to me for a kiss. It was a sweet kiss, a tender kiss, full of emotion and not the heat of so many of our earlier kisses. I would have easily been able to lose myself to it had it not been for Brent coughing to remind us of his presence. "Ooops. And on that note, *vamos!*"

I watched Theo until he exited and then turned to Brent, stars likely still in my eyes, but for the moment focused on my roommate. "Your instincts were right," I told him sourly. "Aaron did get to him, messed up his head good, and he was prepared to walk away from me for the good of the team or some such garbage."

"Ugh," Brent said sympathetically as he flopped in his bean bag chair, turning to face me as I sat up more in my bed. "He was definitely spooked when I tried to bring him back, so I'm glad he came over here and talked to you."

"I think we have his roommate to thank for that."

"Is there anything I can do to help there?" Brent inquired, and I shot him a grateful look.

"No, but that does remind me. I wanted to reach out to Ethan Kim to see about the possibility of him or one of his football friends helping Theo train. I want him to feel better about himself, and if that means he's spending more time with someone else in pursuit of that goal, then so be it." I climbed from the bed and started the process of booting the laptop, then started pacing the room, knowing it would take a bit before I'd see the desktop.

"I could take him with me on my morning runs when you're working the bookstore — if he doesn't have classes during that time. That would help get him in better shape, so if the football guys can do something like box with him, he'd be more agile," he offered, and I paused my pacing long enough to lean down and hug him. I was so grateful for his thoughts. "I'll take that as a yes?"

"It's up to him, but as far as I'm concerned, you're a good option. I know you'll look out for him, even if wanting to avoid that is a big part of the reason he wants to do this stuff." Turning back to the laptop, I noted I was finally at the desktop, and loading up a browser, I waited for FisherFriends to come up. My profile was fairly open, with the vast majority of the lacrosse team and the Pride Council counted among my friends.

Finding Ethan's profile, I zipped him a quick message, letting him know what I was looking to do and asking for his help. He might not be available, but I was sure he had people he trusted that could help build Theo's confidence. Brent had climbed to his feet and read over my shoulder as I wrote, and he nodded his approval at my words. "I think that'll be really good for him."

"God, I hope so. Him coming in here, telling me he'd given serious consideration to breaking us up, scared me half to death. Is it too soon to care that much about him?" Brent patted my back and ventured over to his closet to pull out a lacrosse tank top and sweatpants to workout in.

"It's not too soon if your heart tells you it's time. Remember how I was when I met Misha? Girl blew my mind. And other things." I flipped him the bird and he laughed. "Seriously though, she's a firecracker, you know that. It didn't take her long to wrap me around her pretty little fingers."

"I'm afraid to get too attached," I admitted. "You and the rest of the team are the only things I've had in my life that have stuck around. That he was willing to give up so easily scares me."

"We'll work on his confidence," Brent reminded me. "When he's sure of himself, and sure of his place in your life, there'll be no removing him."

"I hope you're right." I sighed and leaned back in my desk chair, staring up at the ceiling momentarily while he changed behind me. "I've talked to Coach, he said he'd take care of it."

Brent settled into his chair and I turned, finding him putting his sneakers on. "Are you going out like that, or are you not joining in tonight?"

I shook my head. "Theo thinks I should rest."

"But?"

I laughed sadly. "But I'm restless. It's like I've got thirty hamsters running roughshod around my brain, all fighting each other for a chance at the wheel, and there's no sign of relief coming. I'm going to need to take a run or something to clear my head properly. Maybe then I'll be able to rest."

"Do you want me to join you?" I appreciated his offer but I shook my head. "Need the time and space on your own?"

"Yeah. Besides, if I'm going to stumble and trip over my feet, I don't want any witnesses." Brent chuckled and I gave him half a smile. "Go on. Send the boys my regards, and let 'em know I'll be back tomorrow."

"Got it." He climbed to his feet and was out the door with his parka on before I could blink, leaving me alone to my thoughts.

But before I could get too lost in my head, I swung back to my computer to find I had a message waiting for me from Ethan.

EK: Hey bud. Sorry to hear about the harassment your man is enduring. Do you want a Council representative to report it to the deans? In regard to Theo and working out — I can't right now, not with Joshua's difficulties — but I know someone who can. My old roommate, and teammate, Ryan. He's a moose of a guy, so no one will give Theo any trouble working out with him, but he's also got a black belt in Aikido.

Me: Oh nice. So he definitely can help Theo learn to defend himself. That would be perfect. Thanks so much, Ethan.

Ethan's response came firing right back.

EK: No comments about talking to the deans? What are you two going to do there?

I sighed. I wished in that moment that I hadn't opened that can of worms with Ethan, but it was too late to back my way out of the situation now. So I answered.

Me: I'm trying to avoid going to the deans, to be honest. It'll destroy my team, and I can't be responsible for that. There's got to be a way to solve this harassment without getting the school involved...

EK: I dunno. Personally, I'd risk my team, but Joshua is more important to me than a game.

Maybe you're not there yet?

I sat back in my chair. His question, whether an accusation or not, hung in the air, and I swallowed hard. How important to me was Theo? How important to me was the lacrosse team? Which was a higher priority? And if I cared about Theo, why did I even need to ask myself these questions?

Me: Thanks. You've given me shit to think on. And thanks for the suggestion of Ryan — can you put us in touch? I don't think we're friends on here.

EK: No problem. Hang in there, things will get better.

If only it was that easy. Moving away from the computer and climbing to my feet, I ducked into my closet for the moisture wicking hoodie Brent had bought me for Christmas. The black hoodie with a white reflective strip around the middle made it perfect for running at night, and that was what I intended to do. Tossing it on and then heading out the door, it wasn't long before I was in the brisk evening air.

The air was colder than I was expecting, and my lungs weren't prepared for it. Despite myself, I coughed. With a small growl, I took off in a loping run, wishing briefly that I had a set of rollerblades so that I could really make good time. But financially, things were what they were, and I could do little to change my situation until I graduated.

There was a path I could take up into the hills of the Endless Mountains, but I wasn't feeling that. I really didn't want to risk getting lost at night in the cold. If Theo had thought I was sick before, I definitely would be if I got trapped outside for too long.

Instead, I took a right down near the sports fields, knowing they'd be mostly empty with spring sports not yet started for the season. I decided to do laps of the track around the football field, knowing that even while it was boring, it was a good, safe option, and one that would still fulfill my need.

Five minutes stretched into ten, which soon stretched into twenty and then thirty. I sweated up a storm but stayed at a comfortable temperature thanks to the hoodie. The problem was, things were no clearer in my head. I wasn't in love with Theo yet, I realized, or I'd be willing to sacrifice the team for his protection. But I did like him a lot and didn't want to see him hurt, which left me with an unsolved problem.

Eventually, I stopped running laps and moved to exit the field, finding that campus had gotten even quieter while I was running. There were still lights on in the campus union, where clubs were undoubtedly meeting and of course the weight room was still open. But most of the lecture hall buildings were dim — most night courses were done online for public safety reasons.

By the time I'd gotten properly back to The Nic and let myself in, I shivered a bit. It was nothing a quick shower wouldn't solve, but I wasn't sure I was up for the effort. Though I'm sure Theo would argue I set myself up for cold and pneumonia if I didn't...

The shower took little time as my dark, textured hair didn't require much maintenance. A thorough scrub of that and then another of my body and I was good to go, and by the time Brent returned from *his* workout, I sat in a towel on my bed.

"Good run?" he asked as he entered, moving to shed his parka almost immediately.

"Long run," I returned. "Ran around the track until my legs were ready to fall off. But it did clear a few things up for me." I paused long enough that I could see Brent getting ready to speak, and then I rushed out my words. "I don't think I'm in love with Theo yet."

"That's okay," Brent assured me. "Just like it would have been okay if you were. You move in your own time and you do you, Owen. What brought that line of thinking on? Our conversation?"

"Nah, one I had with Ethan over messages. He kinda threw out that Joshua is more important to him than his team, and in my sitch, he'd already have spoken to the deans about what's going on. It stung a bit."

"I can imagine," he replied sympathetically. "But if Theo isn't more important to you than the team, and I'd like to add the addendum 'yet,' then that's just how it is right now."

"I think I'm scared to put that much faith in one person."

"You put that much faith in me," Brett countered, and I stared at him. "Come on now, Owen. You love me like a brother, just like I do you. You know I have your back. You *are* capable of loving someone, you just need to believe in *yourself*."

Waiting until he'd gone into his closet to change, I did the same with my own closet, only bothering to throw on flannel pajama bottoms with the Roseden logo on them before exiting and heading back to my bed. "I thought I did," I mused.

"Theo's not the only one who needs work on his confidence." Brent had settled into his bean bag chair and reached for his gaming system, but he peered around to gaze at me. "You two can work on that together."

"Maybe," I conceded.

"Maybe my ass." I stuck out my tongue at him and he gave me the finger. "I know your home life sucked, Owen. I can't imagine living on campus year round to avoid being homeless. I know that shaped you into the person you are today, but you don't have to let it define you. You deserve love too."

Sucking down a breath, I looked away, roughly blinking my eyes to try and keep from shedding tears. "Maybe," I offered again, and this time he didn't argue with me.

Instead, he just hit me in the gut. "I love you, brother."

Did I feel it too? Was he right? I took a shuddery breath and then glanced in his direction, finding that he wasn't even looking at me, though he didn't have his headset on yet, either. "I love you too."

"I know." I could hear the smile in his voice. "Even if you aren't sure, I know. You'll get there, Owen. Just give it time."

But how much time did I have when Theo's safety may hang in the balance?

9
Theo

If there was one thing that was for certain, it was that I was going to sleep well tonight. After a morning spent interval training with Brent and now an afternoon being spent with Owen's friend Ryan Burton to help me learn how to defend myself, I'd exercised more today than I had in ages. And when it came down to it, that was good for me, something I needed to do. I really didn't want to gain the frosh fifteen and give my parents another excuse on why I shouldn't come back here in the fall.

"Have you ever hit anyone else before?" Ryan asked as we stood in front of a punching bag, gloves on both of our hands.

"Not really," I started. "Unless you count kneeing a dude in the balls because he was trying to get down my pants."

Ryan cringed and crossed his legs slightly. "While a good tactic, that probably won't help if you get into a fistfight. At the very least, your opponent will likely be *expecting* you to go that route. So I want you to put your entire body weight into trying to punch this bag."

Nodding, I focused on his words, trying to wind myself up and hitting the bag as hard as I could muster. Unfortunately for me, it barely moved, and I sighed in frustration. "Who me, weak? Not hardly."

One of those big gloved hands settled on my shoulder. "Patience, young one. We'll get you there. We'll have you using your size to your advantage, since you'll likely have a lower center of gravity than most guys you might battle."

I tilted my head thoughtfully — it had never occurred to me to view my slight frame as an asset rather than a liability. But Ryan was good at getting me to think of things in a different light, and I was already growing to appreciate that about him. "Should I be getting lower, balancing on my feet differently, anything like that?"

Looking me over, Ryan suggested, "Throw another punch and let me watch again. I was mostly looking at the force of the blow that last time and not into your overall stance." Nodding at his words, I hit with my left hand this time, making a bit more headway with the bag, but still making me feel like I punched a brick wall.

As I watched, he shifted himself around away from me, and then threw a punch of his own, the bag moving with a solid *whomp* noise. "Your feet are different than mine," I noted immediately, and he nodded.

"Yeah, you need to widen your hips out a bit, work on your balance. Your feet were too close together initially, so you weren't able to get much force behind your blow. Not only that, you would have been easy for a bully to knock over, too." I made a face at his words and tried imitating his stance, shifting around on my feet until he gave me a thumbs up. "Try again."

With my stance wider, I again wound up for the punch and was pleased when the bag moved a bit further than it had initially. "That was better," I said happily.

"Yep, but we can still improve it," Ryan told me. "Your elbows are out like wings before you extend your arms. They need to be tucked in closer to your body."

"Like this?" I tucked my arms in closer, so my elbows were neatly against my rib cage, and turned more to face him. When he nodded, I couldn't help but grin. "I'll get this yet."

"You will," he promised. "And once we get you rolling, you'll be a lean, mean fighting machine. Not that I would encourage you to go out looking for fights, but you'll be able to defend yourself if it ever comes down to it."

My entire face had to be lit up with my smile. The thought that no bully, like Aaron, could intimidate me any longer was a beautiful thing indeed. And the fact that Owen had thought to get this sort of training for me just endeared him to me further. I was falling hard for that teddy bear, and it was only a matter of time before those three words slipped off my tongue.

"The final step to getting a good punch in is to pivot off your back foot and push your body forward. Your punching motion should be straight and compact, not wild and stretching across your body like you'd see in movies or whatever. Did you ever play baseball?" I shook my head. "Okay, because it's a lot like setting up to take a swing. Same motion. Since that won't help you though, watch me again."

This time Ryan almost painfully slowly set himself into starting position, then adjusted his arms. Finally, he again made the motion to punch, but did the entire thing so slowly that I could watch his hips pivot and propel his body weight forward — but not so much so he was off balance. When his gloved hand hit the bag, it again made a soft thud. "My turn now?" I asked.

At his nod, I spread my feet, waiting for his confirmation before continuing. With my elbows tucked in, I suddenly pivoted and launched my body forward, throwing all of my weight into making contact with the bag. I was truly pleased when the bag seemed to move farther and made a noise. Not the *whomp* that Ryan was able to generate, but a noise nonetheless. "Attaboy! We'll continue to refine your motions, get you going with both hands, but you have the foundation now."

He continued having me throw punches against the bag, which he held, for the better part of ten minutes before encouraging me to stop. I leaned slightly against the bag, huffing slightly for breath but still grinning. "I wish I didn't have to do this, y'know."

"I'm not totally sure I understand why you do," Ryan admitted. "One of your boyfriend's teammates is giving you trouble because you're trans? That just seems...inane. Childish, even. But what do I know? I'm just a big dumb jock."

I snorted at him. "Big dumb jock my ass. I've heard you're headed to MIT next year. Last I checked, MIT was pretty fucking selective about who they let in."

A sheepish grin crossed Ryan's face. "Guilty as charged." The grin faded after a moment, though. "I still don't understand why this Aaron kid feels the need to torment you. Or his implication that the entire team has a problem with you. Not that I'm best buds with the lacrosse team or anything, but in working out around them, I've never gotten the sense they've got some sort of group vendetta against you."

I tilted my head, then shrugged. "My roommate thought that he might be attracted to me, but angry that I'm male and not female. But even if I was female, I wouldn't want anything to do with him — he's got some pretty whacked views on a woman's place in this world we live in."

"One of those?" Ryan asked, and when I nodded, he made a noise of disgust. "Your roommate might be onto something though." He removed a boxing glove to glance down at his smartwatch. "I actually need to split. I need to head back to my apartment to clean up, then it's off to Cordelia Russell College to help a pretty little cheerleader with her Calculus."

I wrinkled my nose — I was looking forward to my math requirement about as much as I had my foreign language one. "Better you than me. See you again this time next week?"

"For sure." He bopped my still gloved hands with his one gloved hand and then winked. "Don't go wandering into the weight room without me. I don't want you kicking my ass when we meet again."

I threw back my head and laughed as Ryan moved to exit, dropping his gloves in a box near the wall of bags. Tugging mine off and moving to follow suit, I glanced at my watch and noted that Owen should probably be wrapping up his workouts for the day. Grabbing my phone from my sweats, I sent him a quick message.

Me: You still around the student union?

It took him several minutes, but eventually I got a response.

Owen: Yup. Just finished. You here too? You want to hang out? Brent is heading over to CR to visit his girlfriend.

An open opportunity to make out some more with Owen? Yes please.

Me: Yep, I'll meet you at the front door, okay? I want to be your little cuddleslut tonight.

He didn't respond to that, not immediately. It wasn't until he met me at the door, coming up behind me and wrapping his arms around my hips, that I got to hear his chuckles. "Cuddleslut, hmm?"

"Oh yes. I'm a total slut for your cuddles." Tilting my head back to gaze up at him, I smiled when he looked down at me. "Let's walk together." I moved to grab one of his hands, and we walked off side-by-side, heading to The Nic. He was still chuckling when we arrived at his building, and as he let me in, I snuck a kiss. "I'm glad I amuse you," I whispered against his lips.

"You really do," Owen confirmed as he nuzzled against my neck. Soon we were in his room, and he flipped the TV on while climbing into his bed, indicating I should follow. When I gave him a curious look while glancing at the TV, he explained, "Hockey night. Brent turned me on to the game. He's a big fan of the team in DC."

"Ooooh. Hockey. I know there's a team in Boston; my dad follows them. Not like fanatically or anything, but there's some black and gold memorabilia in our house." After shedding my parka and the hoodie I'd worn to work out in, I climbed into the bed alongside Owen, letting him pull me into a kiss. "Hello," I breathed to him.

"Hello yourself," he growled, and soon a hand threaded into my hair, holding me to the kiss. It was hot being wanted like that, and it made me shiver in desire. Pressing hot, open-mouthed kisses to my lips, it was easy to feel his rising desire, and I wondered just how far we'd go tonight.

Pulling back from him slightly, I tried to cool us down a little bit to get a handle on things and rested my forehead against his. "Who's playing tonight?"

Owen's pupils were blown wide and he was still trying to kiss me. "Hmm?"

"The hockey game. Who's playing?"

It took him almost a minute to process my question, but when he finally did, he sucked in a deep breath and only then answered. "Boston and New York. I'm not big into hockey, but I prefer the team from New York, because they're closer."

"Then I'll root for them, too." I let our lips come together again but could feel him hesitate just slightly, and I pulled back to assure him, "I want you too, I'm just not sure how far I want to go tonight, okay?"

"Okay," Owen whispered between kisses, and it didn't take too long for the heat, the passion, to rise again. His hand threaded back into my hair, his tongue lapped gently at mine, a fleeting touch that was such a tease that I trembled against him. "Like that, huh?"

"Y-yeah," I babbled, my body so pliable that I was like putty against his. I couldn't help myself, I rocked my hips against his, and his moan was so loud, I wondered if his neighbors couldn't hear him. "Shuuuuush."

"Yeah, you try to hush when your boyfriend has your dick pinned and rubs against it. Not. Fucking. Easy," he growled, and to prove that point, he jutted his hips up against mine so I could feel what I was doing to him, a hard cock poking me in the pelvis.

I panted for breath, not just because he turned me on, but because I was also nervous. Owen seemed to sense that though and loosened his grip on me, letting me readjust myself on his body, letting me pull back a bit. "Thank you," I whispered against his lips.

"I'm not going to force you to do anything you don't want, babe," Owen assured me, and in that moment, I was sure I loved him, but I didn't dare say it. It was too soon, too much, and I'd for sure scare him away if I did. So I nuzzled his neck, kissing and sucking lightly at the skin, not so much to leave a mark, but to make his skin feel electric.

He must have liked what I was doing, because he started to repeat it on me, causing my eyes to flutter shut in pure bliss. "That...feels amazing." His teeth scraped against the sensitive skin of my neck and I almost lost my mind right there. Turning my head, I captured his lips in a kiss; this time I took control and, taking what I wanted, pushed my way into his mouth.

Owen made a growly noise deep in his throat but this time made no effort to hold me tight to the kiss. I threaded *my* hand in *his* hair instead, and he made a surprised noise. "Theo..."

"Mmmhmm?" I tugged his lower lip between my teeth, nipping at it lightly, his moan music to my ears. "Something I can do for you?"

"Goddd. Don't stop." I had no intention of stopping, but it puffed up my ego to have him begging me not to. Soon I was kissing all over his face, his eyes, his nose, and especially his lips, just teasing little fleeting kisses, trying to make him feel me everywhere.

I could feel his dick still poking me, harder if somehow possible, and I had a brief thought about offering him a blowjob, but I wasn't even sure *how*. So rather than pursue something I wasn't entirely comfortable with, I brought a hand down between our bodies to rub it against his sweats, almost giggling when he whined and bucked against my touch.

"Theo," he warned, but I didn't care. I wanted to pleasure him, and I could handle stroking his dick, clothed or unclothed. But first, there was the matter of his shirt. I pulled my hand away from his dick to push up at his T-shirt, until he sat up to give me easier access to do so. "What are you doing?"

"I'm going to touch you. And probably make a mess. But I think you'll find it will be worth it."

"Are you sure?" His hand stilled mine before it could go back between his legs again, wide eyes staring at me.

My response was to grab his cock through his pants and give it a squeeze, making him whine in pleasure. My mouth dropped next to his ear and I made a growly whisper of my own. "Yeah, I'm sure. You're gonna look hot losing your mind."

His wide, pleading eyes showed that he really wanted his pants off, and after a moment of consideration, I went to remove them, again with a little bit of resistance from Owen. I could tell he was conflicted, his dick wanting one thing but his brain yelling at him to slow down for my sake, but I was operating at a speed I was comfortable with, so it was all good.

I had to tug his shoes off first before his pants came off, but when they did, I could see his dick straining against his boxer briefs. "God that's hot," I told him, and he made a whiny noise again, much to my amusement. "My sweet teddy bear is a sexy teddy bear too."

Finally having some mercy on him, I rid him of the boxer briefs, gazing down at his dick as it stood at attention. It wasn't my first time seeing one, but it was in this type of situation. I took my time to admire the length of flesh, drawing my hand over his skin and stroking him slowly, trying to remember what I'd seen from the porn videos I'd watched. He was long and thick, like something out of a movie, and I had the sense that if we ever did have sex, I'd need a lot of lube to feel comfortable.

"I've never held one of these before," I murmured at him. "It's heavier than I expected." Owen's only response was a tortured sounding groan, and he bucked against my hand slightly, urging me onward. I couldn't help the chuckle that slid from my lips, and I whispered to him, "Okay okay, I get the hint. Less talking, more touching."

I almost wished for an instructional video at that moment to ensure I got things right, to ensure Owen ended up satisfied. I varied the amount of pressure I applied, continuing to stroke over him. By the way he was panting for breath, he approved of what I was doing. So I kept at it, letting my nails just barely bite into his skin and humming in approval when that earned me a low whine. "More."

Nodding, and trying to interpret what his one-word, growly plea was for, I kept my hand moving, the stroke a bit harder, the touch a bit faster. His hips were rocking up with every stroke I made now, and by the feel of his quivering dick, it wouldn't be much longer before he lost his mind. "That's it, my bear. Come for me," I cooed, trying to get him off.

Owen made a strangled cry and then my hands and his stomach were coated with a warm, sticky liquid — I kept stroking him until he wasn't spurting anything out any longer. Only then did I pull my hand away and shift to lean down to kiss him, though I pulled away in relatively short order because he was still trying to catch his breath. "Ohmygod," he whispered as he slowly came down from his high and I just grinned at him. "That was amazing."

Looking at the stickiness on my hand and his stomach, I told him, "We need to clean up. You're a mess." He managed a low chuckle and made a vague gesture towards his desk, where I realized there was a box of tissues. Grabbing a handful, I made quick work of the cleaning process, tossing the whole mess in the trash before giving him another grin. "Liked that, did you?"

"Babe." Owen shook his head, at a loss for words. "Please tell me I can return the favor and get you off. I would like nothing more than to make you hoarse from screaming tonight." I shivered at the thought while considering my options. I could resume just snuggling and making out with Owen, or I could let him touch me where I'd never let anyone before.

Biting my lip, I let him see the indecision in my eyes and he kissed my nose, quietly trying to reassure me. After another minute's worth of hesitation, I whispered, "Make me feel good. Please."

"You don't have to ask twice," he assured me, and his hand slid up to rid me of my T-shirt. Before he made any motion towards my pants, he slid down my body slightly, lowering his lips to my chest and biting lightly on a nipple, twisting the tiny nub between his teeth and making me shiver in delight despite the lack of any sensation there. It was more about what he was doing than what I was feeling, and he was doing something amazing.

Still, I reached for his hand, bringing it to my pants, so that he'd get the hint that I wanted as much as he had. He was a bright man, my Owen, and soon my sweats were down around my ankles, leaving only my boxers in his path. I arched up when his hand ghosted over top of my boxers, begging him, "Please."

He wasn't half the tease I was, or at least he was choosing not to be in that moment. I didn't even have to tell him where to touch me; he seemed to just know as his hand slid under my boxers and stroked over the bundle of nerves that made my body electric. My legs opened wider, giving him better access, and I whined when his touches weren't as rapid as I would have liked. "Patience," he whispered from my chest before he slid up and captured my mouth with his own, silencing me further.

Thanks to years of testosterone, I had a small dick, and Owen was stroking it, a finger tracing tantalizingly along my front hole. I gasped into his mouth when the finger slid inside of me, and I bucked up against him; he shifted a hand to bring it to my hips to keep me under control.

He continued to touch and tease and stroke and thrust, over and over again as he made me progressively more mindless, my body trying to thrash on the bed but failing due to his superior grip and weight. I'd never had someone else try to pull an orgasm from me, and the feeling was so foreign it was almost uncomfortable, but not in a bad way. Pulling my mouth back from his to whine, my head hit the pillow hard, my eyes starting to roll back in my head. "Give it to me," he instructed, and I couldn't deny him even if I wanted to.

The orgasm hit me like the most epic wave in the ocean, crashing over me and nearly drowning me, leaving me gasping for air. My eyes fluttered shut as I tried to catch my breath, and Owen brought his hand up to his mouth, licking it clean as I shuddered harder. "Fuck."

"Eventually," he murmured, and I managed a slight nod. "Let me put my boxer briefs back on and we'll cuddle, okay? You wanted to be my favorite cuddleslut, so it behooves me to oblige you."

I drew my eyes open to give him a lazy smile. "That sounds amazing." I watched him pull his boxers back on and pull the covers up and over us. I curled up so that my head was on his shoulder and my hand over his heart. My heart was still beating rapidly, my whole body still blissed out a bit, but I wouldn't trade that feeling for the world.

I wouldn't trade Owen for the world.

10

Owen

In the weeks since Theo and I had become more intimate — and he'd taken up boxing with Ryan — I'd noticed a more confident Theo. He was becoming very adept at simply ignoring Aaron when he glared or sneered at us, and he proudly held my hand at every opportunity. I was proud of him, but more than that, I found myself feeling ways I couldn't quite explain. The closest I could come was the song I'd sent to Theo, 3 Doors Down's "Your Arms Feel Like Home."

He was beginning to capture a part of me that I'd never shared or even wanted to share before, a part of my heart and soul that I'd long kept guarded away from anyone who could hurt me. And maybe Theo could and would still hurt me somewhere along the line, but I trusted him more and more as each day passed. I wasn't willing to say I loved him yet, but that was more of a me issue than a Theo issue.

Brent had taken to telling me, "Goodnight, brother, I love you," each night before we went to sleep, and I couldn't always bring myself to reply back in kind. I felt strongly for him because he was closer to me than anyone on this earth, but as with Theo, love, even the fraternal kind, scared me.

So I threw myself into lacrosse, where I could use my restless energy in an aggressive fashion. We'd played our first game, against our rivals at Binghamton State University, and won fourteen to six. Having Theo there watching and seeing him in my lacrosse hoodie, which he swam in, made me extra happy.

But that didn't stop Aaron from trying to cause a disruption on the team, despite my conversation with Coach about *him* actually being the disruption and him harassing Theo. Any time there was a moment of silence in the locker room, he'd run his mouth about what a distraction Theo was, and how disgusted he was that a non-athlete was being allowed to wear one of our hoodies. Most of my teammates seemed to ignore him, but there were a few players, mostly frosh, who listened with keen ears, soaking up everything he had to say.

It was frustrating to say the least, as was Coach's unwillingness to take any sort of action against his precious faceoff specialist. More than likely, it was that he didn't want to run afoul of Aaron's parents and grandparents, but the whole situation sucked donkey balls, and I didn't like it one bit.

I think part of it was the team's general inaction when it came to Aaron. Sure, he had his followers, but even those who didn't seem to agree with him weren't doing anything to stop him. I guess since it wasn't their significant other on the receiving end of the harassment, they didn't care? It gave me second thoughts about how I viewed the team, but still, they had my back, even when one of the Binghamton Rivermen uttered a racial slur in my direction. All sorts of penalties were called in the wake of that particular scene, and quite a few were on my forwards, who tried to coldcock the guy.

Buried in my hoodie and curled up in my arms, Theo glanced up at me. "You're awfully quiet."

"Just thinking," I told him. "Nothin' to be worried about." I gave him a lazy smile, but I was aware I wouldn't be able to hide behind the distraction; the frustration was in my eyes. The question was, would he call me on it?

"That explains the smoke," he deadpanned, and I yanked on the pulls of the hoodie until only his nose was showing through the hood. "Hey!"

"Hey yourself," I teased. "You started it."

Theo swatted my hands away, grabbing for the pulls and then loosening the hood up until his face was fully visible again. Leaning in to give me a light kiss, he murmured against my lips, "You're so mean to me. I don't know why I put up with you."

A bolt of fear ratcheted through me, the thought of him walking away just enough of a blip, but I tried not to show him that momentary panic. Instead I continued to tease, moving to nip at his lower lip and tug on it with my teeth. "Cuz I make you hot. And bothered. And sexy as hell."

"Well, you're sexy, there's no denying that. I don't know so much about me." I gave him an incredulous look. "You're biased."

"So? And you're not?" I countered, and he shrugged but curled closer to me, ending up with his hand over my heart. I loved it when he did that, but I wasn't going to admit it. It would be opening myself up too much. It was easier to communicate physically.

"Maybe I am," Theo conceded, and I snorted. "Fine. I totally am. But can you blame me? Have you looked in a mirror lately?" I flexed and pretended to kiss one of my biceps, earning me a light swat from my boyfriend. "Maybe I shouldn't be encouraging you."

"That's not what you were saying the other night," I growled, and those blue eyes I adored darkened a shade, growing hungry. "Yeah, you like it when I talk dirty to you, don't you?"

"I like it when you talk sweet to me too," he reminded me, and I could feel the blush creeping up on my cheeks. I couldn't tell if he was trying to put me in my place or was teasing me, but it was embarrassing, regardless. "I'm just saying, we're not just all about the sexytimes. There's more to us than that."

"Yeah, true," I agreed, but still I grew quiet at his words, drifting back into my head again. I think I wanted to love him, and maybe that was where I was at this point, but how could I feel something I'd never before experienced?

"You've gone thoughtful on me." A hand came up and cupped my cheek, and I leaned into it automatically, purring slightly when his thumb glided over my skin. "Maybe you're not a bear, maybe you're a kitty." I made a disgruntled noise and he laughed, but he didn't stop touching me, and for that, I was grateful.

"Just a lot to think about these days. You. The team. Classes. Work. I hardly have a spare moment to breathe." After a moment, I realized that could be viewed as a complaint, and I amended myself. "I wouldn't change any of that, except maybe the job, but I need that to survive, so it can't go anywhere, no matter how much I might want it to."

"Good, I hoped you weren't regretting spending so much time with me." His thumb slid over my cheek again and I nuzzled his hand, letting my eyes drift shut momentarily. Theo had such a light touch, it was easy to get lost in it, to just focus on feeling and nothing else.

"Never," I swore to him, and I drew my eyes open again to find him beaming a smile at me. "Spending time with you is one of the best parts of my day."

"Same for me." He leaned closer to give me a soft kiss then pulled back again, settling his head on my shoulder but tilting his head to gaze up at me. "Is there anything I can do to make things easier for you?"

I thought about his question for a minute before shaking my head, telling him, "No, I don't think so. I knew what I was committing to when I signed up to play lacrosse and when I took the job in the bookstore. You could even say I knew what I was getting into being your boyfriend. Maybe not the Aaron aspect of it, but I'm not sure anyone could have anticipated that."

Theo's face went sour. "I wish he'd just...climb the mountains and fall off them," he muttered, and I tried my best to bite my lip and not chuckle at his words, even though I *did* agree with him. "Seriously. He's a total thorn in my side. Even if I don't let him get to me as much anymore, that doesn't make him any less annoying."

"I know. And I've talked to Coach about him and..." I shrugged a little bit. "There doesn't seem like there's anything he can do. Or at least is willing to do. I'm not sure what to say or do to convince him otherwise. But maybe he's not who we should be talking to about this stuff?" I bit lightly on my lip, already hating the idea of going to the deans, but knowing at this point if things were going to remain unresolved, it would have to come down to that.

"You don't want to go to the deans," Theo responded softly, "so we won't. We'll deal with this on our own. Besides, it's not like he's tried to attack me or anything like that. Just playing head games and that sort of shit. I don't think it'll escalate."

"No, me neither." I sighed in unrestrained relief at the thought of not going to the deans at this point and reached over to run my hand through Theo's hair. As he usually did, he pushed back into the touch then snuggled against me more, making a happy little noise as he did so.

We both remained quiet for several minutes as we just cuddled and enjoyed each other's company, neither of us needing to be anywhere else and content to just be close. Brent was in the room as well, but he was playing video games with his headset on and wasn't likely to interrupt unless he needed to go to the bathroom or something.

When Theo leaned up to kiss me, I didn't stop him and instead actively leaned into the kiss, enjoying the way our tongues journeyed around each other's mouths, feeling my temperature rising from the simple action. Not everything needed to be about sex, but there was also something to be said for having a significant other that could make me horny.

Pressing his face against mine, so that his mouth was near my ear, Theo whispered, "So when's the next time Brent goes to visit Misha again? Because I'm thinking maybe next time, instead of using my hand, I use my *mouth*. Would you like that?"

It was too bad he couldn't feel just how much I liked the idea of that. My dick responded with interest almost immediately, leaving me shifting a bit uncomfortably on the bed. "Only if you're sure you're ready for that."

"Won't know until I try. I can't promise I'll be very good, but I know you'll taste good." I groaned; he was trying to tease me and he was being downright evil about it.

Turning towards him, positioning our faces so we were eye-to-eye, I whispered back, "Maybe it's time I give you a taste then." Theo's eyes widened at the thought, and his mouth made a little 'O' shape as he gaped at me. I think he liked the idea, but he had no clue how to respond to it. "You're cute when you're all ruffled like that."

The hand on my chest lightly smacked me, not enough to cause pain, but enough to get my attention. "We'll see, okay? I'm not saying no, I'm just..."

"I get it," I assured him. "It's a trust issue, and a body space issue and...yeah. I'm not going to push you though, babe, I've promised that and I mean it."

"Eating me out is hardly an indignity to me though," Theo noted, and I bit back a chuckle. "It's just going to be new sensations, because while I can certainly play with myself, and do, it's not like I can put my mouth down there. I'm not *that* flexible."

"I would pay good money to see it if you were," I teased, as much to lighten the mood as anything else. His eyes danced when they met mine, and he made a motion to smack me again.

"I bet you would," he murmured, and this time I did chuckle. He could be cheeky when he wanted to be, and tonight that was clearly the case. "I think I'll limit my flexibility to trying out a good ol' sixty-nine with you, instead. That ought to make you excited."

I'm sure my eyes lit up at the possibility. "Well, that's one way to accomplish things." I tried to go the serious route, but Theo saw right through me and swatted me lightly again. "Ow. Quit that!"

"When you quit being a brat, I will," he retorted. "But I do think that would be a good way to do that, truly. You get your taste, I get mine, and we're both *very* happy with the end result. Course, you'll probably have to yank me up the bed after the fact because I'll be too boneless to move, but I think that's a cross you're willing to bear."

"Oh yeah. I think I can handle bringing you back up into my arms for post sex cuddles." I stroked my hand through his hair again, smothering a chuckle when he headbutted my hand. Some things were predictable, and his reactions to me touching his head were one of those.

"That's good, because I *really* like cuddling with you."

"I never would have guessed," I teased, and I grabbed his hand before he could swat me again, covering it with my own. "Gotcha."

"Hrmph," Theo protested, though only mildly. He shifted closer so that his head was closer to my neck and he kissed me a few times, but not enough to rev me up. "Owen?"

"Yeah, babe?"

"I think," he started, and then his nerves seemed to get the better of him, and he pressed his face more against my neck. I stroked his hair, trying to reassure him, remind him he was safe, and he took a deep breath before spitting it out all at once. "IthinkIloveyou."

I blinked, his words hitting me like a punch in the gut. It hadn't occurred to me, though it should have, that he would fall in love with me. I wasn't expecting the rush of emotion, the impact of his admission. Nor was I expecting the pain of the guilt that I couldn't repeat the words back to him.

The awkwardness hung in the air like the smell of dirty socks, sucking the air out of the room and leaving even our holds on each other tinged with something I couldn't quite define. It wasn't good, it wasn't even comfortable. I wanted to reassure him, but I didn't know how. "It's okay," he eventually whispered.

My shoulders drew tighter. "I'm sorry," I finally said, and it felt inadequate. I felt inadequate, like I didn't deserve this ball of sunshine that came into my life and filled me with joy. Why couldn't I love him like he loved me?

He rolled more to the center of my chest, so that he was balanced on top of me. Pushing up on his hands against my shoulders, he leaned over me, staring down at me until I tried to look away. It couldn't have been more than a half a second later that his lips captured mine, sucking the air out of me in a good way but leaving me clinging to him like he was a buoy, keeping me afloat.

My arms wrapped tightly around him, holding him so close I briefly wondered if he could breathe. He held me to the kiss until I pulled back, half asking, half stating to him, "This doesn't change things."

"No," he assured me. "It doesn't. How we feel about each other doesn't have to be interconnected. I just wanted you to know I loved you. I didn't mean to upset you."

"You didn't upset me." I sighed, rolling my head around trying to work out sudden kricks in my neck. I was getting stressed, even frustrated maybe, with how this evening was progressing, and I almost just wanted to be alone, even though that would solve nothing.

Theo made a *tsk* noise at me. "All this tension," he ran a finger along my face and neck, before continuing, "says otherwise." He pressed his lips against mine again, but only for a second. Then he pulled back and moved to climb from the bed. "I'll give you space to come to grips with this. But we're okay, I promise you that."

I reached for his hand before he could get too far away, tugging him back closer and into another gentle kiss. "I care," I told him. "It's just not love yet."

Nodding, Theo pulled back again, pausing only to kiss my hand before he moved to put his parka back on. I watched him with sad eyes, wanting to stop him but knowing I needed the space as well. Eventually he exited, and it took a minute or two after he left, but then Brent turned my way, pulling his headset off. "He left early. Everything okay?"

"No," I answered shortly and started to roll away so I was facing the wall and my back was to him, but I should have known that wouldn't fly. Within seconds, Brent was at my side, tugging lightly on my shoulder, pulling me flat on my back.

"Oh no, we're talking. Tell me what happened."

I didn't want to answer. I didn't want to admit what had happened, that I had probably scared Theo away despite his assurances that we were okay. But finally I whispered, "Theo told me he loved me."

Brent seemed to understand immediately what the issue was and he nudged me over on the bed until he could sit on the edge. "That tends to go better when both parties feel the same way. I guess he didn't know or realize that?"

I closed my eyes and still tried to roll away slightly. "I don't know," I answered hoarsely. "I just know I feel like I let him down so badly, and I know there's not a damn thing I can do about it. I can't tell him I feel something I don't."

"I know. It's a push sometimes to even get you to admit how you feel about me."

Wincing, I still nodded, admitting to him, "Love scares me."

"Because of how you were raised." It was a statement, not a question, and I reluctantly nodded. "You do realize that at some point, there's going to be someone in your life, maybe it's Theo, maybe it's not, and they're going to be there for the long haul. You won't have to pack up and leave them."

"How do you know that?"

"I don't. I have faith it'll work out that way. I choose not to doubt it. It's much easier to deal with life if I don't let doubts eat at me," Brent murmured, and I looked at him and sighed.

"My life hasn't worked out that way," I told him stubbornly, as if he didn't already know that. "Why should it start now?"

"Why shouldn't it?"

I growled wordlessly. There wasn't going to be a happy ending for me. My life didn't work that way. No one was going to stay with me because I wasn't worth staying with. A lifetime of living out of a plastic bag had assured me of those feelings.

I could feel Brent staring at me, trying to get into my head, and I was bound and determined not to let him in. Not tonight. Not with everything so fucked up and probably beyond repair. "You really believe you don't deserve to be happy, don't you?" he questioned sadly, and I didn't answer. It wasn't that I didn't believe I deserved it; it just wasn't in the cards for me. "I'll leave you alone, Owen. Get some rest. We need you on top of your game tomorrow."

I managed a snort. Even my team, my supposed family, had selfish motivations when it came to me. Did they care about me as a person, or was it just the athlete, my abilities on the field?

These days, I didn't have any answers.

11
Theo

I headed towards the football field where the lacrosse games were held for today's game. Despite how last night had ended, I wanted to support Owen, to make sure he understood I wasn't going anywhere. I did love him, and nothing was going to change that, even if he didn't feel the same way.

With no crowd gathered yet and the teams practicing before the game began, I settled myself at the fence down near the sidelines, watching teammates throw balls back and forth to each other. It didn't surprise me that Brent and Owen had partnered up. It did, however, surprise me when a ball zoomed by me, narrowly missing my left ear, and banged against the metal grandstands behind me.

"What the?" I wondered aloud, turning my head to try and figure out where the ball had come from and how that had happened. After a moment I jogged off to retrieve the ball, finding a fully equipped Aaron had come to the fence waiting for me.

"Give me that," he demanded, and I snorted, underhandedly tossing the ball over the fence, but not near him. "Bitch."

I made a *tsk* noise at him and inquired, "Having trouble with your balls, Callahan? I figured you'd be used to handling them yourself."

Even through the helmet, I could see his nostrils flare, the anger darkening his eyes. He looked like he was going to try and reach over the fence and strike me, but he thought better of it and stalked back toward the field, scooping the loose ball up with his stick and then throwing it to the frosh he was playing "catch" with.

I had to bite back a smirk when he left with me having the upperhand. He definitely didn't like that, but if he'd enjoyed trying to get my goat in the first month or so of the semester, I was now enjoying putting him back in his place every chance I got. A voice called out "Hey, Theo!" and looking up, I found Brent waving at me. I waved back and gazed at Owen, wondering if he'd do anything.

He didn't, not immediately. He stood, also fully geared up, just staring in my direction for the longest time. I offered him a wave, and it was only then his feet seemed to finally become unrooted from their place, and he came towards me, standing opposite me. "Hey," he said softly.

"Hey yourself," I murmured, smiling at him. "Ready to kick ass?"

"Always," Owen answered stoically.

I watched him for a moment, telling him, "You don't have to be over here with me if you don't want to."

"I do want to be," he replied immediately.

I nodded rather than answer with words, offering him my hand over the fence. He hesitated, but only for a second before he was tugging off his glove and reaching for my hand, giving it a tight squeeze, tighter than I expected. He was almost clinging to me, and my heart ached for him, but I couldn't force his head or heart to move before either were ready to do so.

I let him hold my hand for several minutes before I moved to pull it away, seemingly to his chagrin. "I like that hoodie on you." He dragged a finger along my cheek before putting his glove back on, taking a step back and looking back and forth between me and the field.

"Go," I implored him. "I'll see you after the game." That seemed to be all that Owen needed to hear, and he turned to jog back onto the field where Brent threw him the ball once he was close enough. I turned and moved to climb into the stands, going a few rows up then settling down.

There was a chill in the air, and I momentarily wished I'd worn more layers than just the hoodie. But I wanted Owen to see me wearing it, so it was a sacrifice worth making. As I continued to watch, the coach blew the whistle to call the team into a huddle, and for the moment, all you could see was the tops of about thirty black helmets.

Across the field, the team from Scranton College, in their green and gold uniforms, also worked on drills. I wasn't sure what to expect from this game, from this opposing team. I didn't know enough about collegiate lacrosse yet to make an educated guess. From what I'd watched in the

Binghamton matchup, Owen appeared to be very good at his position, but I might be a bit biased.

"Is this seat taken?" I looked up at the soft voice, finding a petite redhead standing beside me, and I looked her over, trying to place why she seemed so familiar.

"No. I know you, don't I?"

She laughed in a devious way. My eyebrows raised and she grinned at me. "I'm Brent's girlfriend, Misha. Misha Smead. You've probably seen pictures of me in the boys' room."

"So you know who I am," I assumed.

"Yep," Misha cheeked. "Brent told me to look for you, described you to a t, even what you'd probably be wearing. And he was accurate. Aren't you cold?"

I grimaced. "A bit, but please don't tell Owen. I wanted him to see me in this hoodie." I lowered my eyes slightly even as she settled in beside me. "I think he needed to see it, to be honest."

A gloved hand moved to clasp mine, and though I was surprised, I didn't pull away. There was something comfortingly familiar about Misha, like she was family I hadn't seen in awhile and we were just catching up. "What's going on?"

I shifted a bit closer to her so that we were shoulder to shoulder, almost in one straight line, and leaned my head closer to hers to admit, "I told him I loved him. He just...froze. I think he not only wasn't expecting it, but he also didn't have any idea how to come to grips with it."

"Oh man, I'm so sorry. That must have hurt." I shrugged. "No, don't play that off. You did a big brave thing and not only did you get no response, but he shut down on you." Misha paused for a moment. "You really are as tough as Brent said you were."

My face heated. "Brent talks about me to you?"

"Not like, all the time? But when you two started running together, he mentioned that. And he's told me some of the stuff you've dealt with here." I made a face and she squeezed my hand. "Nothing to be ashamed of. Some people are just assholes."

"That's Aaron, in a nutshell."

"Well," she started, "to be fair, if I was in a nutshell, I'd be an asshole too." I stared at her; she just giggled at me with eyes dancing. "Sorry, I'm a nut."

"No, it's good. I just wasn't expecting it." I managed a low chuckle but shivered again, and I was surprised when Misha pulled her gloves off, offering them to me. "Wait, you need these."

"I can tuck my hands in the pouch of my parka. You could do the same with your hoodie, but it's not nearly warm enough. Just throw them on for the game, and I'll take them back before we go our separate ways." Still I hesitated until she was snatching them back and putting them on my hands for me, much to my embarrassment.

"Misha!" I whined.

"You sound like Brent," she teased, and I used one of my hands to try and cover my ears, failing miserably as she laughed louder at my expense. "To be fair, he not-so-secretly loves every minute of my torture. Ask him sometime about the paddle..."

"LALALALA! I can't hear you!" With both hands finally free, I tried covering my ears again, but

Misha was tickling me with her now uncovered fingers, and I was left to try and swat her away. "Staaaaaaaaaaahp."

She leaned her head against mine. "Do you have an older sister? Have you ever wanted one?"

"No and no," I replied, though I grinned, because I could see where she was going with her line of questioning.

"Too bad you're stuck with one now." Misha licked my cheek and I flailed around, trying to wipe her saliva off my face.

"Save the tongue for Brent. I'm sure he appreciates it more."

"He does," she said in a dreamy voice. "He so does."

Glancing around as I tilted my head thoughtfully, I let my voice get much lower in question, "Blowjobs. Got any tips? I've watched porn videos, but..."

"You mean you haven't actually had dick in your mouth and the thought is a bit intimidating?" I nodded. "Have you touched his dick at all?" I nodded again. "Okay, good, so you at least know what you're working with. But there's a lot you can do. Are you familiar with the perineum?" Off my shaking head, she continued. "Okay, it's behind the scrotum, goes to the ass. Sometimes called the taint. If you massage that, Owen'll be putty in your hands."

"I like the sounds of that. But what about blowing?"

"I was getting there, sweetheart. Lick anywhere your tongue can get to, any crevice, and especially the vein running along the underside of his dick.

Take his balls in your mouth and suck on them, but gently, because they're sensitive. The actual blowing? More than likely, you'll be using your hand to stroke him off while your mouth tops him. "

Nodding, I glanced at the field for a moment before asking her, "Do you think I should present that to him as still on the table even if we're not back to normal? Or is that just putting a sexual Band-Aid over the situation?"

"I can't really answer that for you," Misha told me, and I sighed. "Honestly, Theo. Because I'm not in your relationship. If it were me in a similar situation with Brent, it would be a Band-Aid, which means I'd be trying to avoid it." She hooked an arm around my shoulders, tugging me closer.

"I should probably let things settle down. Give him time to deal with things however he's going to. Whatever that means for me, us." I glanced down at my hands before closing my eyes momentarily, the brief thought of losing Owen painful enough to choke me up.

Misha's hand slid up and down my shoulder in a reassuring manner, as if she understood where my head had gone in those few split seconds. "Time is a good thing," she eventually told me, and I nodded. "Try not to worry too much, if you can help it. I've known Owen since *we* were all frosh, and he'll pull himself out of his funk. He always does."

I wasn't so sure, because even though I'd known him for far less time, I thought I understood him more, even intimately so. But maybe I didn't? Maybe that was part of the problem? Should I have just sat on my proclamation of love until I could see he was on or close to the same page?

I was poked in the ribs and I glanced at Misha. "Don't you get lost in your head, too."

I faintly smiled at her. "Trying not to. Just psychoanalyzing...well...everything. Wondering what I could have, should have done differently."

"What ifs will drive you batty. If you weren't already there to begin with," Misha teased, and I made a motion as if to swat her, but she just laughed at me. "Seriously, there's always situations for *all* of us that we want to second guess, but it's really not worth it in the long run. It fucks with your head."

"That's for damn sure," I agreed. Closing my eyes again briefly, I rested my head on her shoulder, murmuring a soft warning, "Keep an eye out for flying balls. Aaron already purposefully missed one so it rifled past my ear."

"Immaturity, ahoy, with that one. He needs to get over his bad self."

"It's okay," I countered, drawing open my eyes again. "I threw the ball so he had to go chase it. Told him to do a better job of playing with his balls. He was...unamused."

"Be careful with him," Misha warned. "You don't want to start a pissing match when we can't stand up to piss."

Snorting, I reminded her, "I've been taking self-defense classes from the guys' friend Ryan. Boxing, actually. He's not going to shove me around and get too far."

"It's not the shoving I'm worried about," she fretted. "It's his sanity, or lack thereof. He's a loose cannon. You don't want to be poking someone like that."

I puffed out my lack-of-chest. "I'm a big boy, I can handle myself." She sighed at me. "I'll be more thoughtful about how I deal with him, okay?"

"Thank you. I like you; I don't want to see anything happen to you, especially if it's avoidable."

Not wanting to think about it further, I turned towards the field, where I found the game was about to begin. Aaron was facing off against Scranton's faceoff specialist, and despite all my misgivings about the shithead, he won the faceoff handily, manhandling the ball back to one of the forwards before running off the field to swap men.

My head was on a swivel, watching the ball while trying to keep an eye on Owen as well. He was prowling the midfield, waiting for the ball to enter the defensive zone, where he and Brent roamed. Brent was a defender, I'd learned, and had a stick as long as Owen's. That particular conversation had caused much laughter and crude comments comparing their "stick" sizes, with Owen asserting his stick was wider but still easy to grip.

When the ball traveled towards the Roseden goalie, Brent intercepted it and flung it off towards Owen, who ran it up the field, across the midfield line before lobbing it off to one of his forwards. Owen then returned back to his zone, pacing the area, and I was so busy watching him, I missed the goal that had Misha celebrating beside me.

"You were watching Owen, weren't you?"

"Guilty as charged," I laughed. Still, I rose to my feet and cheered with the rest of the fans on our side. "What can I say? There's nothing quite as sexy as a big, strong man running up the field cradling his balls."

She snorted her laughter. "You could offer to cradle them for him. A nice boyfriend would."

"So would a nice girlfriend," I teased her back. "Cradle, lick, grope. Y'know, all in a day's work."

Misha shook her head, but she was laughing so hard that tears were rolling down her cheeks. I grinned, very content in that moment, and when Owen glanced over, I shot him a discreet thumbs up so he'd know everything was good. Before long, the game had resumed with another faceoff, which Aaron won again, and the Fighting Fishers were off.

When all was said and done, Roseden eeked out the win, fifteen to thirteen, leaving them unbeaten so far for the young season. I was proud of Owen, proud of his teammates, and more than that, I was thrilled when, after the game, he came to find me.

It wasn't an exuberant celebration, it wasn't him trying to tackle hug me or otherwise be overly affectionate, but he did slide his hand in mine and give me a tired smile. He was mine, and that was all that mattered. We'd work through the rest.

12

Owen

For whatever reason, the lacrosse game we played seemed more meaningful than previous games, even more than the championship game we'd played in my frosh year. I don't know if it was Theo's presence, even though he'd been at this year's other game, or what the situation in my brain was, but I needed to impress him, and I think I accomplished that.

He was waiting for me when the game ended, all content smiles and looking cozy in my hoodie. I wasn't sure whether to be happy or scared that he was with Brent's Misha, the spitfire that she was. Lord only knows what kind of thoughts she might put into my sweet Theo's head! But it was easy to slide my hand into his so we could walk back to The Nic for a small gathering before Brent took Misha back to CR.

It was during that time, when we'd long since settled in my bed and were cozied up, that I pulled Theo tighter and whispered to him, "I'm sorry for my reaction yesterday. I just...wasn't expecting you to go there yet. And that's not fair of me, because emotional reactions like that can't be controlled. I really did mean it though when I said your arms feel like home."

"I know," he told me serenely. "But really, I'm sorry for just spilling out how I felt when you weren't ready for that yet. I should have read the situation better and seen that, and I didn't. If I had, we wouldn't be struggling right now."

I flinched, but only slightly. "We're not struggling, are we?" I worried. "We're okay, aren't we?"

"Yes, my teddy bear, we're good, I promise." Theo leaned closer to give me a soft, sweet kiss, lips pressing against lips, no tongue remotely involved, just the barest touch of skin to skin. I found myself clinging to him despite his words and wanting to stay pressed to the kiss, and when he pulled back, I made a whining noise. "It's okay, I've got you."

"I'm just scared," I whispered. "Love is foreign in my world, more foreign than the Spanish in our class. At least that I feel like I can learn. Love seems a much more difficult concept to wrap my head around, with a language that I've never been taught how to speak."

Theo quirked a smile at me, a gentle look, one that reminded me that he cared. "It doesn't have to make sense, Owen. But I understand your fear. When no one in your life ever stays, why would you believe in love?"

Locking eyes with him, I just barely nodded. Pulled from every "home" I thought I'd known, I'd grown jaded long before I hit my teenage years. If not for those police athletic leagues and caring guidance counselors at the schools I attended, there's no telling what would have become of me. I probably had a reserve of anger deep within my soul, but right now, all I was aware of was the fear and the frustrations it was causing in my current relationship.

Grabbing the covers from the foot of my bed where I'd discarded them in the morning, I tugged them over Theo and I, then moved to remove his shirt. He stopped me initially, telling me softly, "No sex, Owen."

"I don't want sex right now," I told him, unable to hide the trace of frustration from my voice. "I just want to be close. I want to feel you." When his eyes locked on mine again, he nodded, and not only did he remove his shirt, he helped me remove mine. Shivering slightly, I pulled him so that we were chest to chest, so I could feel his skin burning against mine.

"I've got you," assured Theo. "I've got you and I always will. And it's okay if you don't believe that right now, because I'll stick around until you do."

I wanted desperately to believe, but the only reaction I could manage was a soft snort, much to my chagrin. I tried lowering my head to break eye contact, but Theo snaked a hand between us until he was able to grab my chin, forcing it upward.

"No running from me. I'm not going to let you push me away, either. I don't know if you'll try and self-sabotage something good, not intentionally but because you don't know any better, but I'll *still* be here."

Sighing, I leaned my forehead against his, trying to lean into a light kiss, which mercifully he allowed. The touch was electric as always, and after a moment or two, I just closed my eyes, letting the feelings wash over me like rain. Maybe he was telling the truth. Maybe he would stay. But would the point ever come when my heart and brain would believe that?

When Brent slipped back into the room a bit later, he went straight to his gaming beanbag chair, pulling his headphones on, and settled into a game with nary a look in our direction. Still, I didn't speak to Theo, I just kept an arm hooked loosely around the small of his back, keeping our bodies tightly pressed together. There was of course a physical reaction to the closeness, but I was ignoring it, and it seemed Theo was as well.

"How long can you stay?" I eventually whispered, before not giving him a chance to really answer and kissing him again harder than before, chasing his tongue with my own, needing in that moment to possess him, needing to feel like he was mine, even if that was fleeting.

It wasn't until we broke the kiss, panting, that he was able to answer, and I was surprised how much his answer warmed my heart. "I can stay the night if you and Brent are down with it. Harv won't mind. I'll just need to run around a bit more in the morning to accommodate it. But I wouldn't mind spending the evening close to you."

"Really?" I didn't want to get my hopes up, but the thought of going to sleep with Theo curled in my arms was a little slice of heaven.

"Really," he confirmed while nuzzling his cheek against mine, such a tender gesture that my heart swelled even more.

"Grab that eraser from my desk, will you? And hand it to me?" Theo raised an eyebrow but obliged my request, and he seemed to finally understand when the eraser went flying across the room, bouncing off Brent's TV screen, which caused my roommate to remove his headset and turn in our direction. "Hi. Question for you."

"Okay?"

"Can Theo spend the night?" I tried not to bite on my lip or cling to Theo too tightly, but the blood left my fingertips and I knew I was holding on to him too tight.

"Sure," Brent agreed easily. "Was that all?" When we both nodded, Brent did as well, and after a moment he went back to his game.

I sucked in a sharp breath in happy surprise then all but pounced on Theo, kissing him hard, my fingernails digging crescent shaped marks into the skin of his back as he trembled and pressed closer to me. I wanted nothing more than to pin him to the bed and own him, but that wouldn't have been fair to Brent — or even and especially not Theo, who I couldn't imagine was ready for that.

But Theo matched my hold nail for nail, skin tight grip for skin tight grip, his tongue sweeping through my mouth as possessively as I'd tried to do to him. There was no denying my arousal now, but I just shifted slightly, trying to reposition the bulge in my sweatpants. Theo must have taken that as a request, because he broke the kiss to whisper against my mouth, "Not tonight. But soon. Promise."

My eyes widened, and I stared at him, wondering what was going to be on offer. Was this a continuation of our previous conversation, of what amounted to mutual blowjobs and dick sucking? Or was he maybe thinking of something... more? I wasn't prepared to ask, so instead I just lowered my head to his neck, sucking lightly on the skin there, leaving tiny little bite marks in my wake.

I could feel Theo shivering, and it just urged me onward, leaving me trailing further down his body until my mouth hovered over his chest, tongue flicking out to lap at his nipples. Before I could move my body any lower to tease his belly button or even just stop there, Theo tugged me back up his body, whispering against my lips in reminder, "Not tonight."

And even though I understood, I hadn't been able to help myself. He'd gotten me so excited with the promise of whatever he had in mind. So I tried to keep my hips a bit away from his, in order not to rev me up further, and I pressed my chest back tightly against his, feeling on fire at the heat from his chest.

One of his hands threaded into one of mine and our combined hands settled between our chests over our hearts, slowing down my rapid heartbeat. There was something reassuring about his hand over my heart, like a drumbeat of awareness that he was there. And even if I struggled with the constant of him being there, I could accept it, in that moment, like that.

"I'm glad you're staying."

"Me too," Theo answered. "Though we might need to get you a cock ring to keep your friend under control."

I couldn't help it, I shivered at the thought. The thought of him controlling my orgasm like that was really hot and something we'd definitely need to explore more at some point. "Fucking tease," I muttered at him, mostly affectionately, and I nipped at his lower lip for a moment before otherwise settling so that we were cheek to cheek.

"That's me," he whispered against my ear with a low laugh. He might have been right about the cock ring though. His voice, his laugh, had some sort of control over me, and I was helpless to control my own actions.

"Hrmph," I grumbled, though with undisguised affection this time, and Theo laughed again, the brat. "Babe? Would you be more comfortable if I was on my back?" He hesitated a moment before nodding and I loosened our hands before shifting and rolling, letting Theo reposition himself so that his head was on my shoulder and his hand, to my joy, was back settled over my heart.

As if seeming to understand the bliss his hand placement caused me, Theo's thumb slid just barely side-to-side, like he was consciously reassuring me of his presence. I made a soft, pleased, noise and hooked an arm over his back, holding him as close as humanly possible, all the while looking over at him and smiling. "We're going to need to strip down to sleep clothes at some point."

"At some point," I agreed. I didn't see the immediate need to rush, however, until he made a teasing point.

"That means less clothes for me. I don't have sleep pants with me, so I'd be down to my boxers."

I made a contented growl. "I don't suppose you'll let me be in my boxer briefs too, will you?"

"Mmm...can you control yourself? Might be safer if you wore these." He pinged my sweatpants, making me swat lightly at him, but otherwise, I conceded his point.

"Truth. Being only separated by skin thin fabric would be too tempting. I'd want to drive you crazy, even with Brent in the room, because I *know* he has earplugs."

"I'm not sure I want to know why you know that." Theo waved off my attempts to explain, and I huffed a little bit but turned to kiss his forehead, reminding him that he was mine and that he was all that I cared about right now.

Theo smiled at me then rolled away, moving to stand, and after shooting a look towards where Brent was blissfully gaming, he stripped out of his jeans and scurried back into the bed, climbing under the sheets so he wasn't exposed. "Nothin' to be worried about," I assured him.

"Says you," he retorted, and I nipped lightly at his lower lip, playfully telling him without words that I knew best even if he wasn't so sure. "He didn't see me though, so I guess you're right."

"I'm always right." I smirked, then shrieked with laughter when Theo's hands settled on my ribs and started tickling. "Okay, okay, maybe not always. But close enough!" He kept tickling until I tapped out and gasped for breath, laughing hard with tears streaming down my cheeks. "Not fair pinning me to the bed to accomplish your goal, babe."

"Funny, you normally wouldn't complain about me pinning you anywhere," he cheeked, and I had a mind to solidly lick his cheek from chin to forehead. I didn't though, I just playfully muttered at him, and he smirked at me and snuggled closer, making me grin like a loon.

I still couldn't believe I'd get to have him in my arms all night, that I'd wake up in the morning and he'd still be there. Would he still be in my arms, I wondered? I guess I would find out. "This is good," I told him.

"Yeah, it really is." Theo laid his head on my shoulder, pressing a soft kiss against my neck. I brought my hand up from his back, bringing it to slide through his hair, feeling rather than hearing him purr in response.

"Now who's the kitty?" I teased, and he tried to tickle me, but I grabbed his hand so he couldn't. With his hands occupied, he took to nibbling my neck, and I shivered. "Don't start something you don't want finished, babe."

He nipped for another moment or two before pulling back, looking at me with wide eyes. "You're still that horny?" he whispered, and I rolled my eyes at him. "I mean, yeah, I can feel, but I didn't realize..."

"I could make you feel the same way," I playfully threatened, and instead of dissuading me, his eyes darkened a shade. "Oh really." Theo's head barely nodded and I let go of his hand, sliding that hand down his stomach and pinging his boxer shorts. "You sure?" This time his head nodded like a bobblehead, and I bit back a grin, letting my hand slide further until it was brushing against his exposed bundle of nerves.

He went almost rigid at my touch, gasping against my neck and sinking his teeth into my skin, clearly trying to remain quiet by giving me a hickey. I had to bite back a groan of my own while letting my thumb move against him, feeling a dampness settling between his legs that signalled his body was responding to my touch.

Panting a little from his bites, I still whispered to him, "You are so sexy when you're coming undone."

Movement out of the corner of my eye caught my attention and apparently Theo's as well, because he immediately tried moving my hand away, trying to get it out of his pants as Brent advanced towards the bed to climb into his top bunk. Once he was up there he peeked over the edge at us. "I've got my ear plugs, but try not to rock the bed too much tonight, okay? I want to be rested for our run in the morning, Theo."

Theo groaned and brought his hands to cover his face, and I could see between his fingers how bright red he'd gone. I only flicked Brent the bird, and with a laugh, he resituated himself back on his bunk, using his hands free setup to turn off the lights in the room. I tried to move my hand back towards Theo's sweet spot again, but this time he wasn't having any of it, grabbing my hand and moving it before it could get too close. "No?" I asked in a voice barely above a whisper.

"No." His face was still crimson, and though he hooked a leg over mine to get closer to me, he was still trying to hide. "I mean, oh my God, Owen. He could have seen us!"

"It's not like we were fucking," I tried to console him, and he just gave me an incredulous look. "Okay, okay, I get it. It was potentially embarrassing. But, babe, you really did look sexy coming undone for me."

I could tell he wanted to be annoyed at me, but a shy smile curled across his lips. "You enjoy touching me?"

"I do," I swore to him. "There's nothing hotter than watching your body coil with pleasure."

"I enjoy touching you too," he replied, and the little tease dragged a hand along the front of my sweats where my bulge was, making me rock against the touch. I growled, and he grinned, ducking his head into my shoulder with a giggle.

Lest he think he was going to get away with that, I pulled my hand away from his and stuck it down his boxers before he could react, giving him a good rub and only then pulling my hand back. His giggles turned into a moan, and from above us, I could hear Brent groan. "Okay, I'm putting in the earplugs!" he called out, and once again, Theo went fire-engine red.

"Turnabout is fair play, babe." I brought my hand to my mouth and gave it an exaggerated suck, letting it drop with a popping noise. The look on Theo's face said he wanted to instigate more, but with Brent so close, he was definitely being cautious.

"Next time he's gone," Theo promised, and I leaned closer to kiss him rather than let him finish. I was certainly agreeable to whatever he was proposing!

13

Theo

Waking up early was my norm, and that didn't change even with Owen beside me. Although it didn't take long after I'd blinked my eyes open for him to do the same, perhaps because I was nuzzling his neck and kissing lightly at his skin. He growled a soft "good morning" to me, and I smiled before I turned his head to chase a proper kiss as my response.

I could feel his morning wood pressing against me, and despite knowing it had little if anything to do with me, it still turned me on. There was something about lying in close proximity to someone aroused that was a real boost to your ego. "Hi," I finally whispered to him, nipping lightly at his lower lip and tugging it between my teeth.

Owen's eyes fluttered shut for a moment before they drew back open, darker than before. "Can you come by later when he's in class? I'd like to take you up on those promises you were making last night."

Pulling back just enough to be able to lick my lips, I asked, "You wanting me to make you a mewling, growling mess?"

"Yes," he answered shortly, before pulling me back in for another possessive kiss that we probably would have continued for awhile if not for the sound of Brent stirring from his bed.

"Shit," I whispered, glancing at my pants on the floor. I wanted to get them on, but did I dare climb out of bed, in my boxers, in front of Brent? Biting lightly on my lip, I stretched and snagged the jeans, pulling them beneath the sheets and then trying to climb into them, all while Owen rolled his eyes at me.

"Y'know it's nothing he hasn't seen before, right? Maybe not on you, but..." I gave him a look to silence him and kissed him hard again before pulling back as Brent worked his way down the ladder, climbing from beneath the sheets myself and rising to my feet.

"Morning, Brent," I greeted him, reaching for my shirt to tug it on. It wouldn't have been the first time he'd seen me shirtless, but I was still self-conscious about my scars.

Owen's roommate rubbed the back of his head with his hand, yawning before he answered, "Mornin'. We goin' runnin'?"

"Yep. Do you want to run like this?" I pointed down to my jeans and the oversized lacrosse hoodie that I was grabbing off the floor, "Or do you want me to change into proper running clothes?"

"As long as you've got running shoes on, it doesn't matter to me what you wear. Well, so long as you're warm. I don't want to have to bring you back to Owen later, freezing cold and catching pneumonia. He'd kill me!"

Tugging the hoodie on, I smiled at him. "I'll be fine." I looked over my shoulder at Owen, who sat up in bed, the bulge, at least to me, no less noticeable than it had been when it had been pressing against my leg. I gave him a subtle nod, agreeing to his plans for later, and then moved to grab my sneakers, dropping into Owen's desk chair to put them on.

It didn't take long before I was laced up and ready to go, and I followed a similarly dressed Brent out the door and out of the building. "Ready?" he asked when we reached the chilly morning air. I shivered, but only for a moment, before nodding my agreement, and he was off, leaving me to scramble after him. Our runs were usually made largely in silence, and this one was no exception — until we'd been at it for about ten minutes and he asked, "Did you two...y'know...last night?"

I almost tripped over my feet before I came to a halt and stared at him. We hadn't done anything, but by his question, could we have gotten away with it? I didn't dare wonder. "No," I eventually answered. "You couldn't hear us?"

"Not with the ear plugs in," Brent confirmed. "And the bed didn't shake at all, not like I'd have probably felt it as soundly as I sleep. I was just curious how brave you were. I know Owen has a bit of an exhibitionist streak."

"Exhibitionist streak?"

"Uh, yeah. He'd totally feel you up with me in the room and not think anything of it. Not to make him sound like a slut or anything, but he's done it before with other people." I scowled. It's not that I thought Owen was a monk before me, but I hated hearing that he'd had boyfriends, and from the sounds of it, had been sexually active with them. "Sorry, I didn't mean to burst the *Owen is pure* bubble."

"Oh, I know he's not pure." Still, I took off at a run, not wanting to think about it, not wanting to deal with it. It wasn't fair of me to get upset that he had a past, especially when that past had nothing to do with me. That's what I kept telling myself at least.

I didn't get far before Brent chased me down, grabbing me by the shoulder and slowing me to a stop again. "Listen, I'm sorry. I never should have asked, and I never should have told you about his past. Please forget this conversation ever happened, okay? I let my curiosity get the better of me, and I'll never forgive myself if in doing so, I hurt my best friend's relationship. I love him like a brother, and getting him to admit even *that* back is a challenge, so I can only imagine what you're up against."

To that, I only gave him a knowing look. He was obviously well aware that words had been spoken but not exchanged. "It'll take time," I finally told him, and getting a bit agitated with everything, I asked, "can we run again?"

"Of course." Brent took off, leading me to scurry after him once more, and we settled into silence for the remainder of our twenty minute run. When it concluded, he gave me a friendly, if sweaty, hug, and we went our separate ways, with me going back to Tucker Hall for the first time since I'd left before the lacrosse game.

I wasn't surprised to find Harv still in bed when I arrived, so I edged in quietly, pushing the door shut with nary a noise. Toeing my sneakers off, I wandered over to my laptop, booting it up while moving to get out of my jeans and hoodie. I intended to throw the hoodie back on, but I wanted clean clothes underneath that, and with Harv sleeping, I could even change underwear without hiding in my closet.

About the time I finished changing and the computer finished all its boot mechanisms, Harv pushed himself up on his bed, staring down at me with a bit of an evil grin. "Nice of you to come home finally. Did you have a good night with lover boy?"

"Things are better, yes. But get your head out of the gutter. Brent was there. I may have a dirty mind, but I'm not *that* bad." Still, I wondered if my cheeks and ears gave away that I kinda was *that bad*.

Harv rubbed the sleep from his eyes then climbed down his bunk ladder, ending up on the ground, barefoot, not too far from my desk. "Your ears say otherwise," he reported, and he cackled when I must have gone more red. "Go, Theo! How far did you two go?"

I ducked my head slightly and muttered to him, "We just got a little handsy. More Owen than me. And that was mostly to get me back because I got handsy with him."

He nodded in appreciation. "Still. You're trusting him with your body. That's a good thing."

"I love him," I countered. "I trust him. He's not going to hurt me."

Harv flicked an eyebrow upwards. "Does that mean that you two are going to do the dirty at some point in the not-so-distant future?"

"I don't know," I started, "but maybe? I'm not opposed to it. Though maybe a little scared because you know I've never done *anything* like that before. And if he uses my front opening instead of my rear, that'll be painful."

He had a wry grin on his face. "Hate to tell you, but the backside'll hurt as well unless he's really good at what he does...and even then..."

I sighed. "Way to help me not feel nervous, Harv." My friend and roommate came closer and settled his hand on my shoulder, giving it a squeeze. "Am I irrationally worried about something that might not even happen?"

"Probably," he agreed. "You say you trust Owen, so if you do, see what happens, let things go as they may, and roll with them. Maybe he takes it somewhere you're more comfortable, like mutual blowies."

I shivered; the thought excited me as much as it admittedly scared me, though Harv was right — mutual blowjobs were definitely in my comfort zone. "I can do this," I finally told him, and even from behind me, I could sense him nodding.

As I went through Anki to do my Spanish studying for the day, Harv turned away from me, presumably to get dressed in regular clothes. He'd gone to classes in his pajamas more times than I could count, arguing that was one of the perks of being a college frosh — you *could* go to classes in your pajamas!

"Harv?" I asked, without looking over my shoulder at him, instead staring resolutely ahead at my laptop.

"Yeah, Theo?"

"What's sex like? Really?" I didn't get an immediate answer, and when I turned my head, I found a half-dressed Harv, sorta stunned, staring at me. "Sorry, was that too much?"

"No, it wasn't, just wasn't expecting it from you, that's all." He finished getting dressed, then moved to drop into his desk chair, turning it to face me. "You've jerked yourself off before, yes? So you've experienced orgasms?"

This time it was my turn to be stunned, though I should have seen the question coming. After a long moment, I managed a tiny nod. I could never bring myself to get off while he was in the room, but in those periods when he had class and I didn't? My toy collection wasn't quite what it should be, but I had enough means to satisfy myself.

"I've almost always been on the giving end of fucking, not the receiving, but I have received. And yeah, pain, but if your partner knows what they're doing, the pleasure will override that before too long. Especially if they're triggering your erogenous zone. I'd dare say you're lucky; yours is on the outside, more easily manipulated."

"Hadn't thought of it that way. A guess that's a plus for my awkward body? Go me!"

"Your body isn't awkward," Harv reprimanded. "It's how you look at it that is." I lowered my head slightly, but only for a moment, because Harv continued down his previous track. "Sex though. Feeling it is intense. I'm not sure there's even words to describe the sensation of something in your hole, filling you up from the inside."

"Intense sounds like the perfect description."

"Just remember that with the right tools, you can be the one doing the fucking as well. Though that's obviously a conversation between you and Owen, about if he's even comfortable doing it that way. One would hope he is, but you never know. Some people are exclusively tops."

Climbing to my feet, I went to my toy box and fished out the one dildo I did own and showed it to Harv. "A step ahead of you on the right tools. Just never used it on anyone besides myself. I'll have to see about getting accessories for it and maybe a few others. Though as you said, assuming Owen is interested that way."

"I know you love him," Harv began as I put the toy away, and I turned to face him fully. "But consider that he may not be your only sexual partner in your lifetime. Not that you want to think about it, but you may break up at some point, despite how you feel for him now."

I shook my head. "Not going there. Nope, nope, nope."

Harv lifted his hands in the air in a "I mean no harm" gesture. "Understood. I won't go there again. Just wanted you to at least think about keeping your options open with your toy supplies."

"I appreciate that," I told him. "But I love Owen, and that's one subject that I don't mind not thinking past."

He made a gesture that could have been interpreted as "suit yourself," but before I could call him on it, he stretched his arms over his head and climbed to his feet again. "I'm going to The Big Dough for breakfast. Can I get you anything?"

"Boston Creme and a large coffee? Let me pay."

"Let me pay, he says." Harv looked amused. "You do remember I've got more money than I know what to do with, right? That the parentals keep the absurd allowance going even when I'm doing things they don't like, like getting a C in my Stats course?"

"I know, I know, I just hate seeing you waste your money on me."

"Okay, that's it, I'm definitely buying," he countered. "You are worth spending money on, and I'll swat you the next time you imply otherwise." I huffed at him, but he ignored me and headed towards the door. "Keep griping, Theo, and it'll be *two* Boston Cremes!"

My stomach would hate me for that, but ohhh, the thought was delectable. Rather than argue, I let him leave and went back to focusing on Anki. I was still struggling with classes, and I needed to get that under control if I wanted to be able to convince my parents that I should stay at Roseden for more than just this semester.

They thought of this semester as a trial of sorts, a "we'll see how things go and then proceed" plan that might mean that they might try to pull me out of Roseden all together, even though I was nineteen now and legally an adult. I was still living under their roof when I wasn't at school, and I'm sure they'd use that to try and influence my decisions.

I should probably mention all of that to Owen, to warn him what my parents might try and pull, but the easier solution would be to buckle down and get my grades straight. Easier. Right. If only schoolwork was easy for me!

14

Owen

Waiting for Theo to arrive at The Nic after Brent had left was like the worst form of torture. He was coming, but he couldn't get there fast enough for me. His barely-there nod from this morning had gotten me through the day, the promise of what was on offer, what was to come, leaving me desperate for time to fly.

Finally, he came into view, and I stood in the doorway until he was close enough for me to hold the door open for him. I barely waited until he was through the door before I was grabbing his hand and scurrying off towards my room. I wanted him, and he'd see how badly once we reached the safe enclosure.

"Eager?" he breathed against my ear teasingly as we approached my room.

"You'll see," I hissed, and I all but pushed him through the door, slamming it shut behind us and grabbing his hand, bringing it down to the bulge in my pants. I groaned, loudly, when he took that as an invitation to squeeze me through my jeans, the denim suddenly feeling way too constricting.

"I think you need to get out of those jeans," Theo murmured, and I was only too happy to oblige, backing away from him and shedding both my shirt and the jeans, leaving me just in boxer briefs that did nothing to hide my desire. I watched him stare at my pelvis and blatantly lick his lips, and it took everything in me not to crash our lips and bodies together.

While I watched, he stripped out of my hoodie — his hoodie now — and T-shirt, with his jeans following thereafter. He'd never been particularly defined when we'd first met, but that hadn't mattered to me. But now, after running with Brent and working out with Ryan, he was starting to build some definition, especially in his arms, and it was just more eye candy for me. "You're stunning," I told him.

Theo blushed but didn't argue and instead asked me, "Bed?"

"Bed," I agreed, and I took his hand, leading him to my bed and letting him flop on it before I climbed on as well, pressing our bodies close together and gasping at how little separated us from being skin on skin. "Fuck, I want you."

Before I had the chance to truly wrap my mind around what was happening, Theo had stripped his boxers, lying next to me in all of his naked glory. But that lasted for barely a minute before he shifted on the bed, repositioning himself so that his head was between my legs and his groin was right in my face. I moaned loudly when he nuzzled my dick through my boxer briefs, and he chuckled, so I did the only thing I could do to retort — I pulled his dick into my mouth and began to suck.

When Theo gasped and pressed more tightly against me, I thought I had him right where I wanted him, but he started maneuvering my boxer briefs down just enough until my dick was exposed. For the first time, and what I hoped wasn't the last, he took the head into his mouth, and I brought my hands to his ass, squeezing tightly enough that there was sure to be fingerprint marks in my wake.

His hands slid over and around my balls, squeezing, tugging, and otherwise providing enough sweet torture that he was easily going to make me mindless in no time. All I could do was continue to attack him with my mouth and tongue, though I did bring a hand from his ass to between his legs, letting a saliva soaked finger edge into his front-facing hole. "Shit!" he gasped, and for a few moments, my dick was forgotten while he writhed.

I smirked, but not for long, because doing so seemed to renew his interest in getting me off, in tasting me, and much to my surprise he was deep throating me, surely hitting his gag reflex but not letting it affect him. I tried to keep from thrusting down his throat and just focused on pleasuring him, tongue working overtime on his dick.

Theo whined when I tongued him with extra vigor, fucking my face while I did the same to him. In the back of my head I couldn't believe we were doing this, that he was letting me do this to him, and I wondered just how far we'd go. Would he let me rub my dick against his until we both got off in a hot, sticky mess? Or maybe, just maybe, would we fuck?

I didn't have time to think too much; he was making me mindless with his teasing. For someone as inexperienced as he said he was, he was doing an excellent job making my toes curl. When I slid a second finger into him, he stroked my taint, making me twitch and involuntarily rock deeper into his waiting mouth.

"Not gonna last much longer," he told me, and I took that as an invitation to pump my fingers harder and deeper, letting my mouth work over his dick. His legs were shaking, his knees were clamped tight to hold my head in place, but still, I persisted.

A swirl of my tongue, flicking it just right, and I could feel the juices flowing and muscles starting to spasm around my fingers while Theo moaned around me. I licked up everything on offer and then sat back slightly, satisfied, waiting until he caught his breath, knowing it wouldn't take him long to finish me off.

It took him perhaps two minutes before he was attacking my cock, gripping it with one hand and stroking it in jerky motions. The stimulation was just about perfect, and the feel of being in his hot, wet mouth was all that I needed. I came with a roar and a stream of cum down his throat. Feeling him swallow around me made me shiver hard.

Once he'd finally licked me clean, Theo climbed up my body, keeping us pressed so close together it was hard to tell where one of us began and the other ended. I captured his lips in a hard kiss full of tongue and teeth, fighting for possession of every inch of his mouth, wanting him to understand and feel deeply that he was mine.

Between the kiss and the feel of his dick against my own, it wasn't long before I was aroused again, rubbing my body against his and whining into his mouth. "Fuck, fuck, fuck," he whispered, and I agreed wholeheartedly. The feeling of our bodies *so very close* and still hot and sweaty from our earlier activities made the movement easy, desirable, and seriously intense.

Grabbing for his hands, I took them both, holding them tightly as I continued to rock my body against his, grinding against him and seeking as much stimulation as I could possibly get. It wasn't a dick up my ass, but feeling my dick edge along his hole without entering was enough of a mindfuck to keep me going. This orgasm wouldn't be nearly as powerful as the first, but the fact that I was going to come twice in a half-hour was still a good show of stamina for me.

We continued to grind together and kiss until it was just too hot to keep our mouths so close and we had to separate, both of us breathing heavily and trying in vain to catch our breaths. Theo squeezed my hand, and I could tell by his quivering legs that he was close again already, and to be fair, it wasn't going to take me long, either. Pulling a hand away from his, I snaked it between our bodies, stroking his dick *just right* until he was howling out his pleasure, his shaking body triggering my second release, spurting along our stomachs and the bed. "Fuck," Theo whispered again, and I couldn't help but agree.

"Tell me you have a strap on," I almost begged, and rather than give him a chance to respond, I told him, "I'd love nothing more than to feel you deep, arms wrapped around my chest, pushing into me. That would be so fucking hot."

He shivered against me and rested his forehead against mine before telling me, "No strap-on. Yet. Just a single dildo that might be able to be strapped in. Regardless, I can certainly afford to invest in toys for us both, and I was already thinking about doing that."

The thought of him spending money sobered me up a bit, and I urged him, "Don't spend money on account of me. I want you to buy things because you want to, not because I asked."

Theo brought his hand up to cradle my face, thumb stroking my cheek. "Believe me, I'll probably be more comfortable fucking you to begin with than the reverse. Just because I *haven't* yet. And I know it's going to hurt, either way you slice it."

I nodded my understanding and nuzzled his hand, murmuring, "Maybe then, if you were going to do it anyways, I could shop with you. And maybe I can chip in."

"We'll see about that." Theo stared into my eyes, almost challenging me to argue with him, and I found that I couldn't, no matter how much I wanted to. Instead, I sighed and leaned my forehead against his. "Babe? We should probably clean up before Brent gets back. And get at least somewhat dressed."

"Yeah. Lemme get the wipes." I slowly pulled away from him, hating the separation but knowing it was necessary. Opening the drawer of my nightstand, I grabbed the baby wipes, giving us both a good wipe down before discarding the dirty wipe in the trash bin. "Better?"

"Much. Not that I mind being covered in you, but that's better suited to a time when Brent won't be back shortly." Theo leaned closer, catching my lips and giving me a soft kiss before he climbed from the bed, blushing slightly as he reached for his boxers to pull on.

"You have no reason to blush; you're gorgeous," I told him.

"As long as you believe that," he retorted, and I rolled my eyes at him. "I tend to find you much easier on the eyes than I do myself, but that's a matter of personal preference."

"Indeed, because I find the opposite to be true." I climbed to my feet as well, fishing my boxer briefs from the bottom of the bed where I'd kicked them off. Pulling them back on as Theo pulled on his, I sighed sadly as I looked him over. "I wish we could have stayed like that forever."

A half-smile curled over his lips. "Someday we will. Even if you aren't sure you believe that yet."

"In time," I promised him, because I wanted to believe it to be true. I wanted to believe I could love, that I could love him especially, that he wouldn't leave, and that we could have a happily ever after that I'd never thought possible before. The smile I received in return at my words lit up the room and made me even more certain that I needed to find some way to believe in love, if not for my sake, then for Theo's.

"Want to cuddle until he comes back from his class?"

"I like the sound of that." I reached out for his hand, pulling him so that we were standing chest to chest and kissing his nose. I laughed when he wrinkled his nose and whispered against his ear, "Do that again and I'll lick your cheek."

"Don't you dare."

Laughing louder, I tugged Theo off towards the bed, climbing in and then opening my arms so that he could fall into them. Even somewhat clothed, I was still burning hot for him, but there could be no more sexytimes until we had more spare moments to ourselves. Theo was getting braver, for sure, but he wasn't *that* brave yet.

"When I go shopping, I'm getting you a cock ring," he informed me, and though I shivered, I also nipped at his neck, little bite marks across the flesh. "Like that, do you? Definitely getting you a cock ring. Definitely, definitely."

I growled, wordlessly, and shifted to capture his lips, sliding my tongue into his mouth with no resistance and fighting for dominance immediately. The thought of him bringing me to the edge over and over again without letting me have release was almost enough to get me off again right there without even being touched. But instead, I focused on the promise, on the kiss, and on getting lost in the wet heat of his mouth.

Tongues tousled and tangled for possession, neither one of us able to claim dominance for more than a few seconds. It was glorious, it was hot, and I brought my hands up to cradle his face, to hold him steady. I was breathing heavily when we separated, and it couldn't have been a few minutes more when the door opened and Brent came in. When he paused inside the doorway, I realized immediately what the issue was — we'd kind of left a trail of clothes to the bed.

"It's safe," I called out, and Theo tucked his head against my shoulder, his blush going to his ears.

"Not sure Theo's ready for me to see the curves of his ass," Brent countered as he nonetheless advanced further into the room, dropping his backpack and moving to settle into his desk chair, turning it to face us. "So should I be offering the neighbors earplugs?"

"Probably," Theo piped up, and I raised an eyebrow at him. "He's noisy." I gaped, and Brent started laughing, and after a moment, I did too.

"You're one to talk!"

"No, I'm one to scream," Theo replied, and his eyes danced the entire time.

"I'm staying out of this," Brent said with a laugh, as he moved to grab his headset and resettle into his beanbag chair.

"I should go," Theo told me, and I legit pouted at him, wondering what was making him feel the need to leave now that Brent was back. The two of them had never had any issues before that I was aware of. He gave me a quick kiss then shifted off the bed, grabbing for his pants and quickly yanking them on.

I turned on my side to watch him, reaching for him when he was close enough to tug him in for another soft kiss, but he pulled away relatively quickly and resumed getting dressed. On went his shirt and then the lacrosse hoodie, and finally, he shot me a sad smile. "You sure you need to go?"

"I'm sure. I've got homework I need to be working on. My grades are still shit."

"I can help you with that," I swore, confident that I could make a difference in his grades.

"You probably can. But not tonight, okay? We can text though." He offered me one more kiss, and before I could form another complaint, he was out the door and presumably on his way to exit The Nic.

Sighing, I moved to climb from the bed, only this time getting dressed in sweats and a lacrosse T-shirt, and I noted that Brent was watching me. "He left," I offered with a shrug and a sigh, and Brent lowered his eyes slightly. "What's that look for?"

"Given that I don't think he just came here for a booty call, I may be responsible for chasing him out," he admitted, and I froze in my spot, staring at my roommate.

"What happened?"

"We talked some this morning during our run. The subject of your past came up, that you'd been with other people, that you had a bit of an exhibitionist streak. He wasn't too keen on hearing any of that. I think he knew in his heart you'd been with other people before him, but that didn't mean he wanted to talk about it."

I groaned. "The last thing he needs to do is compare himself to any of those wastes of my time. I don't want him thinking he's a booty call, as you said, or a short term, like they ended up being. The sex was good, but I sure as shit didn't love any of them."

"Do you love him?"

I paused, surprised I'd set myself up like that. "No," I finally answered. "But I care about him a lot, more than I ever did any of them."

Brent shot me a sad smile. "Sorry if I ruined your night, bud."

I shook my head at him, "Nah, I can always text him or send messages via FisherFriends. Besides, you heard him talking about his grades. Those really do need to take priority. He doesn't need to be putting himself in a position where he's on academic probation or worse. In fact..."

Me: We all good? Just wanted to check since you left here like your ass was on fire.

It took him a good fifteen minutes before he responded, but when he did, I let out the breath I'd been holding.

Theo: Yeah, we're good. Brent's probably already told you what happened this morning. It was just a little awkward and I didn't want to deal. Plus, it wouldn't have been my *ass* on fire.

I smirked slightly, glad to see he was in good humor.

Me: That can be arranged though. That can definitely be arranged. Only when you're ready though, not a moment before. I know you're worried about the pain. You can always light *my* ass on fire, if you'd prefer. ;)

Theo: Let me go shopping first, and then we'll work on that.

Putting my phone down, I grinned. There was something to be said about the promise of your boyfriend sticking a dick up your ass and rocking your world. I couldn't wait until Theo had the necessary supplies and decided to cross that bridge with me. Maybe with me on the bottom he'd be more willing to cross it sooner?

We'd find out, I guess.

15

Theo

It was another lacrosse gameday, this time during the weekend, which meant that Owen was having to take off from work to take the bus ride to Lehigh Valley State College in Allentown. I'd coordinated with Misha to get a ride with her to catch the game, and I was genuinely looking forward to rooting for our boys, even in enemy territory.

It had been a relatively quiet morning spent working on homework and trying to figure out ways to pull my grades up. I'd sent emails to my professors, offering to take on special projects, anything to increase those pesky Cs to more palatable Bs. And while I'd had no success so far, that didn't mean I wouldn't keep trying.

The last thing I planned to do before I headed out with Misha was to check social media to see if there was anything that needed my attention before I went. I had the FisherFriends app on my phone, but it wasn't nearly as intuitive on that device as it was on my laptop, so I cranked the laptop open and waited for everything to load up.

In hindsight, I wish I hadn't checked.

Maybe then I wouldn't have seen the pictures on Owen's page, the ones of him and a *girl* clearly having sex in an at least somewhat public area based on the shots, and I wouldn't have felt sick to my stomach. All the doubts I'd ever had about Owen and relationships in general came shooting back. Was he really ever gay? Did he like women? Was he expecting me to be like a woman, and being able to fuck me like that whenever he desired?

I didn't know what to think; my head was spinning. When Harv came in from a trip across campus to The Big Dough, he said, surprised, "You're still here? What's wrong?"

Rather than answer with words, I showed him the pictures, and I could hear him suck in a stunted breath. There was no easy explanation for these photos, nor was there any telling how old they were. "I'm going to be sick, I think."

"No, don't be sick. Talk to Owen. There's got to be a reasonable explanation for these photos. He didn't put them on there, for one." At Harv's words I checked to see who had and wasn't at all surprised to find that Aaron had. I shouldn't have been stunned, neither that he had access to Owen's page, nor that he'd done something like that. He had no use for me, and any way he could rattle me, he would.

"I can't. He's on the bus to Lehigh Valley. His coach would flay him if he took a call now from his distraught boyfriend." Looking at my phone when it suddenly dinged, I groaned. "And I bet that's Misha. Fuck!"

"Go down and get her, bring her up here, and see what kind of ideas she has. Or just send her to the game on her own. One or the other," Harv told me knowingly, and despite my misgivings, I nodded and went down to the door to greet Brent's girlfriend, pulling her into a hug on her arrival.

"You ready to go?" she asked as she looked me over.

"No," I sighed sadly. "Aaron posted some pictures on Owen's FisherFriends page of him and a girl fucking. And it's messing with my head big time. I don't even know which way is up right now."

"A girl?" Misha furrowed her brow. "He hasn't had a girlfriend since our frosh year. Mary-Ellen, she was a bitch and a half. Only interested in sex, but then again, I think that's all he was interested in from her, so it worked, for awhile at least. Want me to see if that's who it was?"

I hesitated a moment then nodded, ushering Misha through the door and leading her up to the dorm room. Poking my head inside before letting her in, I called out to Harv, "You decent?"

"Yeah, I'm just stuffing my face."

"Good enough," I replied, and led Misha fully into the room, letting her go straight to my computer where the images were still up.

"Oh yeah, that's Mary-Ellen," Misha confirmed immediately, and some small measure of relief swept through me that the photos weren't recent. "I don't know where Aaron would have gotten these photos though. That looks like he's banging her behind the fieldhouse some evening, and

Aaron should have been a senior in high school at that point."

That made me frown, and fret, and I asked in a soft voice, "Could the photos be more recent?"

"You mean, do I think he's pulled a hookup with her recently? I'd have to ask Brent about that, honestly, but he was happy to be rid of her when they broke up. She was too high maintenance for him."

"You should go to the game," I told her in the same soft voice, and she turned away from the computer to stare at me.

"You're not coming? What'll I tell Owen?"

I grimaced again, and after a moment of thought, said, "Tell him I wasn't feeling well. That's not really a stretch at this point, because seeing that," I gestured towards the computer screen, "made me want to be sick. That's more than we've done and it's done a number on my self-confidence and trust. And I know I need to talk to him, but it can wait until he's back after the game."

Misha tugged me into a hug. "I don't think you have anything to worry about, Theo, but I can understand where you're coming from. I'll tell him you're under the weather, but please, please, please get in touch with him sometime today. When he sees those pictures, and realizes that you have too, he's going to freak out."

I had a passing thought that perhaps he should have thought of that before he engaged in such behavior, but that would have been like telling fifteen year old me not to trust the football players in high school when they wanted to get to know me better. Sometimes, we just don't make good decisions, and sometimes they come back to bite us in the ass later. I eventually nodded my head at her, and she gave me one more tight hug before moving to exit.

"I'll text you updates. And maybe stealth pictures of your boy lookin' studly."

I quirked a smile. "He always looks studly; you'll run your phone out of battery taking that many pictures."

Her eyes danced with amusement. "Good to see your sense of humor is still intact. Hang in there, Theo; I promise you things will work out." With that, she was out the door, leaving me with Harv and the pictures.

Silence reigned supreme for several minutes, both while I stared at the photos and Harv finished devouring his muffin. When Harv finally spoke, it was to ask, "So, what are you thinking?"

"I'm hurt, and I'm not sure I have any right to be," I admitted. "I mean, Brent made it clear Owen had relationships before me. It just never occurred to me that some of those relationships were with *women*, not men."

"So he's bisexual or pan. No big. He still cares about you."

"That's what I keep telling myself, but there's a nasty little voice in my head wondering if that's really the case. I won't give him sex, not like that, especially not in public, and maybe that's what he'd want?" Even despite my words, I remembered Owen begging for me to fuck *him*; he wouldn't be doing that if he only wanted me for the female parts I still had.

"I think you know better than that," Harv counseled. "Maybe you'd feel better if you had a declaration of love from him in your pocket, instead of just knowing that he cares a lot."

"Maybe," I conceded. "It's just..." I waved my hand at the photos, the obvious lines of his ass visible, and the woman's skirt hiked up high enough you could nearly see her chest. I couldn't see his dick, but that's likely because it was buried inside her. I don't know why that grossed me out so much, but it really did make me feel like I was going to be sick.

Harv came up behind me and reached over my shoulder, closing out the window that the photos were on, despite my feeble protests. "You were turning green. I didn't want you spraying the laptop. Do I need to get you a trash can?"

"No, I think I can keep my stomach under control, I just..." And still I flailed, struggling to find words to explain what I thought, what I felt. It hurt, but it was more than that. It was almost like I expected more of Owen, like I thought better of him than to fuck some random—even if he was dating her at the time—behind the field house, where he could get caught, as he had.

"It's a shock, I know. It shocked me too when you showed it to me, and I'm not dating him. Given that her body is similar to yours in some ways, there's an extra layer of almost...deception?... that has to make it feel more painful. You put Owen up on a pedestal, and through no fault of your own, he's gotten knocked soundly off of it."

I stared at Harv as he spoke, tilting my head thoughtfully before finally giving him a resigned nod. Whether I liked it or not, that did sound accurate, and once I'd given my heart to Owen, I'd trusted him completely. This *did* feel like a betrayal, even though it wasn't one. I could have asked him about his past at any time, found out about his complete sexual preferences, and maybe even been made aware that there was the possibility of pictures like the ones that were posted existing. But I didn't, and that was on me as much as it was on him.

"Now you're wondering what to do next, right?"

"Yeah," I agreed. "Should I have gone to the game with Misha, pretended like this never happened? Or do I deserve a while to pout and come to grips with it all before I get in touch with Owen and talk it through with him?"

"I'd say pout now, while he's at the game, and then text him, asking him to let you know when he's back at his dorm, because you want to stop over. Then clear the air. Tell him you were upset and why. Give him a small ration of shit for not telling you about his ex-*girlfriend* and that he used to fuck her in public places. And then forgive him and move on. Because if you really love him, in the general scheme of things, this is something small."

"Aaron wanted it to be something big, clearly, or he wouldn't have posted it. And I still want to know where and how he got the pictures. But you're right, that doesn't matter; it's not important. What is important is that we don't let something like this split us up, because that's letting Aaron win."

"Exactly. And you know once Owen realizes what's going on, he's going to be freaking the fuck out. Because he does care about you, and the last thing he'll have wanted to do was hurt you or publicly embarrass you or anything like that. No doubt he'll be worried sick until he does see you and hears from you himself that everything is okay."

"Yeah," I breathed. "I just need to calm down and settle my stomach." I paused, turning things over in my head before adding, "I don't know how I would have handled this if it had happened in the first few weeks of our relationship. Actually, yes I do. I remember Aaron trying to make what you called a devil's deal with me and cowing to him."

Harv nodded even as he moved to climb up to his bunk and gazed down at me. "You're a lot stronger, mentally and physically, than you were when you arrived here. Not only has the relationship with Owen been good for your confidence, but so has the friendships you've made through Pride Council. I mean, you can always send a text to Ethan or Beau to get their thoughts on things, too."

"I wonder if Ethan would know where those pictures came from?" I stared up at Harv then moved back to my computer, composing a message to the football player. There was no guarantee he'd be able to come up with anything.

"Does it really matter?"

I tilted my head thoughtfully. "No, not really. Though I imagine Owen will want to know, because that's an invasion of his privacy. And her privacy for that matter. It may even be against the law." With that thought in my mind I pulled the images back up again, downloading each of the images and screen capturing Owen's stream, where it clearly showed that Aaron had posted the images.

"I hadn't thought about the legal aspect of it, but you're right. Though, would the town police even arrest a Callahan?"

Scowling, I finished gathering evidence and shut the computer down. "I don't know. They'd probably try and say it was all a big misunderstanding."

Harv snorted. "Officer, I don't know how the pictures got posted from my computer. They just magically posted themselves."

I settled on my bed, grabbing my stuffed bear and then staring at the upper bunk, even though Harv couldn't see me. "Thank you, my friend. You've helped me not only see the light with this, you've improved my mood immensely."

"That's what friends are for," Harv countered.

It was going to be a bit before the lacrosse game started on campus radio, so I adjusted my pillow and closed my eyes. "I'm gonna nap before they play, I think."

"Do that," he encouraged me. "I'll wake you up in time for the game, so at least you'll know the results."

With his promise in my ears, I settled down under my blankets and let my body relax. This day hadn't started out well, but I was determined not to let it end that way.

16

Owen

I should have realized there was a problem when I didn't see Theo and instead caught Aaron smirking. I should have known something was up. But I listened to Misha when she told me that Theo was under the weather and I brushed it off. It was only when we got back on the bus to go home, when I found a message from Theo telling me we needed to talk when I got back to my dorm, that I became alarmed, and I asked Brent if Misha had told him anything.

He hesitated a long while before he answered, and even then it was in a voice full of caution. "I'm not supposed to tell you until we're back at campus. In fact, now that you've seen that message from Theo, I'm supposed to confiscate your phone, reply to him for you, and not let you have it back until we're back."

He snatched the phone out of my hand before I could fully react, and though I tried to swipe it back, he kept it out of my reach, using an arm to bar me from stretching and grabbing. "Fucker," I muttered, and after a few moments of seat wrestling, I finally gave up, sitting in my seat and sulking.

I wanted to know what was going on. I wanted to know why Theo needed to talk to me. I was pissed, worried, and more than a little bit afraid. What happened today?

When we finally reached campus, I changed so fast that it was quite possible that my clothes were on backwards. Brent struggled to keep pace with me, but he chased me to The Nic, where he finally handed me my phone. "Now can I reach out to him?"

"You're going to want to pull up your FisherFriends page on your laptop first."

I raised my eyebrow at Brent, wondering what was so important on that site that warranted my attention over reaching out to Theo. But I booted the old school laptop up, tapping my foot impatiently while waiting for it to reach the desktop. By the time it had the browser window open and on my FisherFriends page, I'd changed again, this time into sweats and a lacrosse T-shirt. But I couldn't believe what I saw. "Are you fucking kidding me?"

"No. Aaron posted it, sometime before we all left for Allentown. And Theo noticed it before Misha was supposed to pick him up. I know they talked, and he's supposed to be calmed down now, but I'm going to visit the library for a while...while you two talk."

I closed my eyes, trying to wrap my head around it all. That little fucker had posted pictures that he had no business even having, let alone posting, and Theo had gotten upset. Maybe he was no longer upset, but Aaron had at least initially had his desired effect — Theo hadn't come to the game. "Thank you," I finally told him, and I waited until he left with his backpack before I texted Theo that I was back at The Nic and I'd be waiting at the door for him.

On a blustery day like today, odds were that Theo would make the walk pretty quickly and not waste any time. Within five minutes he was standing in front of me, looking me over before giving me a soft kiss. "We're okay," he informed me, and I sighed, knowing at some point that likely hadn't been the case.

Threading my hand into his, I led him up to my room, explaining once we reached it, "Brent left for a while, said we needed some time to ourselves to talk."

Theo stepped closer, reaching a hand up to cradle my cheek, which I leaned into. "I meant it when I said we're okay. You don't need to be all gloom and doom. Yeah, I freaked out when I saw it, but in talking to Misha and Harv, I calmed down." His thumb dragged across my face, and then he asked, "Did you really fuck her outside?"

I lowered my head slightly. "Yeah, I did. She matched me for fearlessness; it was her one redeeming quality. She was willing to go anytime, anyplace, anywhere. Including behind the field house at dusk in the fall."

"That's not me, you know," he informed me, and I nodded.

"I don't need it to be you. I'm good with you the way you are," I countered.

Theo tugged me towards my bed, actually going so far as to push me down into it before he climbed in and joined me. When he had me effectively pinned to the bed, he stared down into my eyes. "Why did you never tell me you had past girlfriends, too?"

I wanted to look away, but I held his gaze, telling him honestly, "It didn't seem important. It had nothing to do with us, and before you start fretting about your so-called girl-parts, it had nothing to do with those, either. You're a man, you're my boyfriend, and who I dated in the past shouldn't affect our future."

"You're right," he agreed, "but it really threw me for a loop to find out you had girlfriends, perhaps because of those girl-parts you mentioned. I wondered briefly if those were what attracted you to me." I started to interrupt, but he finished before I could. "Then I remembered you *begging* me to fuck you, and I realized you don't care what parts I do or don't have."

"Exactly," I said, relieved. "Yeah, you and her both have front holes, but that's the end of your similarities. She was..."

"I don't care what she was," Theo murmured. "I care about you, and what you think, and how you feel." He paused for a long moment then added, "I think you could probably have Aaron arrested for posting those pictures. Due to the explicit content, what you *can* see."

"That seems extreme." As much as I loathed Aaron, getting him arrested would affect his placement on the lacrosse team and would cause a schism on the team. And if there was no issue between Theo and I, was it really necessary to get the police involved?

Theo stared at me. "You realize your ass is on broadcast for the world to see? Is that really something you want a prospective employer seeing? You fucking a girl?"

"I already have a summer job lined up," I told him stubbornly.

"Did you hit your head today or something?" Theo shook his head at me. "I'm sorry, but you're being stupid. You're risking everything over someone who isn't worth your time."

"Exactly, he's not worth my time! So why would I stir the pot and call the police and make a scene? I'm sure I can either hide the post, or failing that, get the school IT team to remove it."

Theo rolled off me, moving to stand. "Then do it."

"Really, right now?"

"Do I matter to you at all?" Theo countered.

"Of course you do!" I rolled to stand as well. "But I don't see what that has to do with me removing or not removing that post."

"Idiot. Of course you wouldn't. It's always your team, your team. Your team is your family. If your team is such a good family, why have they done nothing to stop Aaron? Why are they letting him continue to harass me? Why has your coach not respected the school's zero tolerance policies?" He turned, making his way towards the door.

"Wait!" I said, and Theo stopped, turning to face me. "I don't want to get the police involved, but I'll hide the post if it makes you feel better."

"You just don't get it." Before I could fully comprehend what had happened, Theo was out the door, and my attempts to plead with him, cajole him back into the room, went nowhere. I gave up by the time we reached the stairwell and went back into my room, settling down on my desk chair and sighing to myself.

Reaching for my cell phone, I texted Brent, letting him know he could come back, that Theo had already left. That would bring questions, but I didn't answer the texts and instead just stared blankly at my closed closet door. Why was Theo so bent out of shape about whether or not I called the police? It wasn't like it affected him or something.

When Brent slid through the door sometime later, the first question off his lips was, "What happened?"

I turned my head slowly in his direction, trying to keep my emotions in check, and told him, "He's upset that I refused to call the police on Aaron, that I don't see an urgent need for having the photos removed from my page. They're embarrassing, yeah, but taking action on them seems like letting Aaron win, right?"

Brent continued into the room until he'd settled on his beanbag chair, shifting it to face me. "I don't know," he began slowly. "I kinda see both sides of this. I'm sure Theo is looking at it as you being unwilling to protect him from Aaron..."

"I am willing to protect him from Aaron!" I protested and Brent sighed at me for interrupting him.

"As I was saying, because by not doing anything, you're showing you aren't taking Aaron seriously as a threat. I think you need to talk to the coach again, because something needs to be done. Maybe if he's punished on the field, that sends the message that his behavior won't be tolerated?"

I put my head in my hands. "I don't want to get the team involved," I muttered. "I don't want a me versus him mentality in the locker room; I don't want people picking sides."

"Do you want Theo?" Brent asked bluntly, and I nodded. "Then you don't really have a choice but to act."

"Why is he putting me in this position?" I whined.

"Because he loves you, and he trusts you to not put him in a vulnerable situation. People are going to talk about those pictures, and there will be those who will assume you're only dating Theo because of his female parts. And Theo has to bear the burden of that, not you. The quicker you resolve the situation, the less abuse Theo has to tolerate."

Brent's explanation made sense, but still the whole mess frustrated me. I didn't want to be the team drama llama, I wanted us to continue to be the family we'd been my entire time at Roseden. "The team is a family, right?"

"Compared to what," Brent countered. "The team is a toxic wasteland, an unhealthy environment for anyone different..."

"They stepped up and defended me when that guy called me the n word," I interrupted.

"Perhaps so, but your relationship doesn't go over well, which is why Aaron even has support in the locker room. It's a whole culture where toeing the line and being the same are expected, and anything else is viewed as a disruption. What kind of 'family' is that, honestly? Where you're made to fit in, in order to receive their love and protection?"

"It beats anything else I've ever known," I answered quietly.

Brent rose to his feet and came to where I sat, pulling me to my feet and wrapping his arms around me tightly. "You deserve better than that," he whispered in my ear. "You deserve my love, Theo's love. People who genuinely care about your good times and your bad times. I wish you could see that." He pulled back and stared at me, even as I tried to look away. "You deserve love, Owen."

I ended up wrapping my arms around him and hugging him back, resting my forehead on his shoulder and trying to come to grips with everything. I had choices to make, it seemed. Choose wrong, and I stood to lose Theo, which I didn't want to do. Which meant that there wasn't really any choice at all — I needed to talk to Coach as soon as possible about the invasion of my privacy and also make an attempt to hide or otherwise get rid of the photos on my stream.

"Do you need me to give you space again so you can call Theo back over here?" Brent questioned, reading my mind.

"Would you mind?" I ventured, even as I pulled away from him and went to the laptop to see about hiding the photos.

"Not at all. I'll just go to the floor lounge and do a bit of studying. That way I'll be able to see Theo when he leaves. If he leaves. If he's spending the night, just text me so I know to come back, alright?"

Brent's hands settled on my shoulders, giving them a squeeze, before he pulled back and went to grab his backpack again. I turned and looked over my shoulder at him, turning things over in my head before I told him quietly, "I love you too."

He cracked a smile at me, even as he continued towards the door. "I know, even if you aren't always sure. And I think you're getting there with Theo too. Maybe you're even already there now." With that thought hanging in the air, he exited the room, but at least this time he wasn't that far away.

I texted Theo, asking him to come back, and after figuring out how to hide the message *and* block Aaron from posting any more messages on my stream, I got up to head to meet Theo at the door. He was just arriving when I got down there, and I pulled him into a tight hug, telling him quietly, "I choose you."

"What do you mean?" he asked, even as he pulled away but went to grab my hand, letting me lead the way up to my room.

"I mean that I...care about you a lot...and chose you over all this other nonsense that's been going on. I've hidden the message and blocked Aaron from posting again. I'm going to talk to Coach and let him handle the situation. If he doesn't, I'll think about going to the police, okay?"

Theo tilted his head thoughtfully and finally nodded, entering my room once I opened the door and pulling me back into another tight hug. "I choose you too."

I wasn't prepared for the rush of warmth that filled my heart at his words, the clench of something real. It caught me completely off-guard, and I clung to him tighter, not willing to let go. "Lie with me?" I asked, and he nodded. We ended up curled in each other's arms, forehead to forehead, and I pressed my lips lightly to his, telling him softly, "This is where we're supposed to be."

"I'm not letting you go, Owen. You've got me for keeps."

For keeps sounded really good. Now I just needed to convince myself to believe it.

17
Theo

It had been a good several days. I'd gone to another lacrosse game, though at Brent's suggestion, I'd been low-key about it. I'd not worn the lacrosse hoodie and instead bundled up in my parka with the hood pulled up. Owen knew I was there, and that was all that mattered. He was a stalwart in the midfield as always, and the Fighting Fishers won again, seventeen to ten.

It was a Friday again, and I'd spent much of my morning cramming for our Spanish quiz. With Owen's help, my Spanish was certainly improving, but I wasn't certain that I'd remember the proper tenses when pressed. I had to give it my best effort though — my grade point average depended on it. When I'd studied about as much as my brain could hold, I'd texted Owen that I was ready for a pickup and went to the front of Tucker Hall to wait for him.

He arrived within minutes, backpack on and a happy smile on his face. His gloved hand slid into mine, and we were off to class, a little bit early, but not so much so that we'd have to deal with Aaron — more than likely at least. When we reached the classroom door, I followed Owen inside, taking my gloves off and stuffing them in the pockets of my parka, waiting for him to leave his recorder at the lectern before following him to "our" seats in the middle of the classroom.

Aaron was there, I could feel his glare, and I resisted the urge to turn and give him a cheeky little finger wave. I wanted to, but Misha's words about poking the angry bear echoed in my head. Aaron was causing enough issues as it was; the last thing I needed him to do was try and escalate further.

I'd talked to Ethan over the course of the week, and while he wasn't certain where Aaron would have acquired those pictures, Brent had been able to shine a light on that instead. It seems an outgoing senior had taken them and gifted them to the freshman most like him — Aaron — for use when the big Black man caused issues.

It still dismayed me that Owen thought that group was a family and was resistant to bumping the apple cart. Didn't he realize his mere existence on the team as a gay Black man was enough against the grain to be a disruption to their perfect little boxes? But I couldn't, wouldn't push him. He needed to come to that conclusion in his own time.

Still, I worried about his psyche when it did all come crashing down, particularly with his past. It would feel like he'd lost another family, and that would be devastating to him. It would be on Brent and I especially to try to keep him upright, to remind him that he was loved and better off without them.

Once the professor arrived, he went over the instructions for the quiz before distributing it, having Owen move over a seat further away from me, presumably under the guise of preventing me from cheating, considering I had the worst grade of the two of us. I could see Owen was a bit agitated by the move, but I shot him a smile, and he held my eyes for a moment before nodding.

The quiz, mercifully, was multiple choice. We had sentences to fill out, and we had to pick out the correct tense of the word provided in order to complete the sentence. I closed my eyes at several points to play the sentences out in my head, to try and make sure they sounded correct before I made my choices, and some twenty minutes after we'd been given the quizzes, they were collected.

Owen took his seat back beside me again and leaned his head against mine, asking under his breath, "How do you think you did?"

I waved my hand in a so-so manner, before answering, "Okay. I'm sure I made mistakes, but we'll see when he grades those. I hope I didn't do too poorly. My parents will kill me if I bomb this class."

"I won't let that happen," he told me confidently.

"I know." I grabbed his hand and gave it a quick squeeze before turning my attention back to the front of the room, where the professor had gathered all of the quizzes and was preparing to start lecturing. I opened my text to the section where we currently were and pulled out one of my highlighters, a bright pink one, starting to go over the text as he reviewed it.

It was a busy class, no time for idle hands, or less, idle chit chat. Periodically, though, I'd feel Owen settle his hand on my knee reassuringly, reminding me of his presence, and I'd smile every time he did it. The hour flew by, and when we were done, I gathered up my books, watching as Owen did the same.

Something brushed past me, moving me slightly out of the way, and a voice snarled, "You're disgusting." I didn't have to look to know it was Aaron, and I purposefully ignored him, just turning to Owen instead.

"Don't forget your recorder," I reminded him, and he playfully rolled his eyes at me.

"Like I'd really forget that?"

"You might if I distracted you," I teased, and I leaned up to give him a soft kiss, feeling his arm wrap around my back to both hold me steady and close. After a moment, I pulled away, laughing, and he grinned at me. "Okay, recorder."

Grabbing my gloved hand again, Owen snagged his recorder, tucking it into his backpack before we continued towards the exit. "My room?"

"Yeah," I agreed happily. "Study and snuggle?"

"I think studying is overrated, personally. Let's just stick to the snuggling," he teased, and I laughed, tucking up closer to his side as he led us off to The Nic. I found the stairs much easier than I had when I'd first walked them, and I practically bounced up them in anticipation of getting up to Owen's room. "Someone's excited."

I snorted but giggled. "That's usually you and your little friend. Speaking of which," I leaned so that I was right up against his ear, "I got you a cock ring. For y'know, the next time we decide to mess around."

Owen sucked in a breath then groaned before opening the door. "Breeeeent. Tell Theo to stop picking on me," he called out, and his roommate laughed at him.

"Good job, Theo."

"Thank you, I thought so too," I deadpanned, and Brent and I both cracked up while Owen tried to casually adjust his pants. "Poor babe." I pinched his ass through his jeans, making him jump, and that only made me cackle more.

Brent watched us with a happy smile for a moment before grabbing his headset and tossing it on, then turning his attention back to his video game. With him properly distracted, I tugged Owen closer by the front of his jeans, stretching up to kiss him. "Mean to me," he mumbled against my lips, and I laughed softly.

"But I love you," I countered. "That has to count for something."

His eyes softened. "It counts for a lot. More than you know." Gently, oh so gently, he stripped me out of my parka, draping it over his desk chair before doing the same with his jacket. With us safely down a layer, he tugged me off to his bed, curling so that we were side-to-side, face-to-face.

Threading my leg between his, I reached out to grab his face in my hands, cradling his cheeks and leaning closer for a kiss, closing my eyes and just relaxing into the gentleness. There was no rush, no heat, just two mouths connecting and getting to know each other again. It was, for that moment, perfect.

"How long can you stay?" Owen whispered to me, and I tilted my head thoughtfully, trying to figure out the answer to that question.

"If I head back to my dorm at some point and grab my books and you help me study, I could potentially stay the weekend. Assuming Brent doesn't mind, of course."

"I can't imagine he would — in fact, I bet he'll probably spend some time with Misha this weekend. Which would mean you could show me that cock ring you bought." His voice was growly by the end, and I had to bite back a grin. I had him *that* excited, and the cock ring wasn't even anywhere nearby!

Rather than make any motions to leave, I instead pulled back from Owen slightly to strip down to my T-shirt, feeling it too warm for my sweater. He followed my lead, and soon I was able to slide my hands up and under the soft cotton and rest my hand over his heart. He looked so content at that point I wanted to stay there forever.

Owen chased my lips for another soft kiss, but this time with a bit of tongue action, nothing outrageous, just two lazy tongues meandering through the other's mouth. I bit back a moan and just pressed closer to him, needing to be as close to him as possible. When his hands threaded into my hair, I moaned into his mouth, my eyes fluttering shut briefly. "I've got you," he assured me.

"I know," I breathed against his lips. "You chose me." Maybe he wasn't taking that as seriously as I was, but right now, that was as close to a declaration of love as I was going to get out of Owen, and I was okay with it.

"Always." He nuzzled my nose with his own, making me sigh happily, and I leaned my forehead against his, staring into dark brown eyes. I was so in love with this man, and I was certain I'd feel that way for the rest of my days. I was safe with him, protected, like no person or thing could even remotely try to harm me.

We cuddled as afternoon shifted into evening, and my stomach finally started to grumble, hoping for food. Owen laughed at me but nudged me to get off the bed, and when I obliged, I glanced back at him. "Sandwiches?" I asked, because it was what I was in the mood for, and it was only a short walk across campus.

Grabbing our top layers, Owen handed me my sweater while pulling on his hoodie. "That works for me." He slid past me to go over to where Brent was, and after a quiet conversation between the two, Owen nodded and accepted some money from Brent. "Just before we head back, I need to grab Brent a sandwich. Don't let me forget!"

"I'll try not to. But when we're heading back from the sandwich shop it would be a good time for me to go back to Tucker Hall, talk to Harv, and pack up to spend the weekend. Sound like a plan?"

"Okay," Owen agreed easily. He held out my parka for me to slide into it and then climbed into his own jacket, both of us putting our gloves on so we'd stay warm outside. It wasn't even above freezing, so I'd have been wise to put on a hat, but I didn't have one.

Once we left The Nic, we headed hand-in-hand to the student center, where the sandwich shop was, and ordered our food. I ordered a six inch turkey with cheddar, mustard, mayo, pickles, and extra salt and pepper. Owen opted for a steak and cheese, with American cheese, toasted in the oven, with red and green peppers. We sat at one of the tables to dig into our meals, and Owen looked me over curiously.

"Mustard *and* mayo? Really? And there I thought you were somewhat normal, Theo."

I stuck my tongue out at him. "I'm perfectly normal, thank you, and it's these kinds of sandwich shops that developed this habit. Their norm is to put mustard and mayo on unless you tell them otherwise, and I grew to like it. The flavors mix well together."

Owen smirked at me. "If you say so. I still think you're weird."

"What does that make you?" I countered. "You're the one dating me. Clearly your taste is questionable."

"I think my taste is quite good." Owen smiled. "A good sandwich, a great boyfriend, what more could a guy want?" My face flushed, and I ducked my head down to focus on my sandwich, but Owen's hand reached across the table to cover mine. "Nothing to be embarrassed about."

"On the surface I know that, it's just sometimes I can't believe a great guy like you wants to be with a guy like me. You've got so much going for you..."

"And so do you," Owen interrupted. "You're smart, sexy, with a wicked sense of humor. You're not afraid of putting me in my place when the need arises. You don't necessarily understand lacrosse, but you're out there every game, cheering your heart out for me. Seriously. What more could a guy want?"

"A big dick on your partner?"

Owen made a dismissive gesture. "Yours is detachable, not one size fits all. I mean, the beauty of your situation is you can pick different size dicks for different situations. Depending on our moods even. And again, I say, lucky me."

I had to smile at him at that point, because he really was hammering home how much I meant to him. Yeah, we were still missing those three words, but they'd come at some point, and then we'd be truly complete. Digging back into my sandwich, I kept my eyes on him as he did the same to me. "If we're not careful, we're going to make a mess," I teased, and he laughed.

"My aim is pretty good," he countered, "and my mouth is like a hoover, which you will attest to." I shivered rather than reply, giving him a hungry look, which made him smirk. "Yeah, I thought you might agree."

"You're just evil." I took the last bite of my sandwich and balled up the wrapping paper, aiming for the trash can and missing horribly. With a grumbled sigh, I rose to my feet and picked up the paper, throwing it away properly, and then turned to face Owen. "Don't forget to get Brent his sandwich."

"Oh yeah!" Owen abandoned his half-eaten sandwich to get back in line and start a new order, and I sat back down, waiting for him to return. Thankfully, the sandwich line always moved at a good pace, and it wasn't more than five minutes later when Owen returned. "So we go our separate ways for a bit, then you'll text me when you're on your way over to The Nic so I can meet you at the door?"

"Sounds good," I agreed. I watched him as he ate, watched as his Adam's apple bobbed up and down, becoming transfixed by it.

"You're staring. Am I dessert?"

"Not tonight. Not with Brent there."

"Bummer," Owen deadpanned, and I chuckled softly. "I'll make sure he goes to visit Misha this weekend then."

"I bet you will," I teased. It didn't take Owen long to chow down on his footlong, and when he went to toss *his* wad of paper wrapping away, it went perfectly into the trash can. "Ass."

Rather than respond, he grinned and offered me his hand, tucking Brent's sandwich under his other arm. "I'll walk you to Tucker."

I leaned my temple against his shoulder as we walked, watching the cold air we exhaled form into little puffs of clouds in front of us. When we finally reached my building, he gave me a kiss and a wave, and I went inside, bounding up the stairs two at a time to reach the room I shared with Harv.

"Good day?" my friend questioned as I bounced into the room, and I nodded, tossing my backpack on the floor and shifting to unload and reload it with the books I'd need to study from.

"Very. If you don't mind, I'm going to spend the weekend with Owen. Sounds like Brent is going to spend some time with Misha, so we might have some time to ourselves."

"Ooooh." My roommate's eyes lit up. "Better pack that cock ring." Predictably, I flushed a bright red, and Harv laughed at my expense. "In all seriousness, I'm happy for you. I'm happy you found him and that he takes such good care of you."

"Me too," I agreed, before turning to my closet to pack a few days worth of clothes into a duffel bag. I didn't need a lot — another pair of jeans, a pair of sleep pants, and a few T-shirts — I could always steal his hoodies if it came down to it. Nodding with satisfaction, I zipped up the duffel, tossing it and my backpack over my shoulder. I was weighed down a little bit, but the walk was only a short one, so it wouldn't make too much of a difference.

Harv bounded over to give me a hug, telling me, "Enjoy your weekend. I'll try not to be *too* envious. But if anyone deserves it, it's you. Keep in touch though."

"You know I will," I promised. "In fact..." I pulled my cell phone out of my parka pocket and sent a quick text off to Owen to let him know I'd be on my way shortly before putting the cell phone back into a pocket of my backpack. "See you Monday morning."

Harv moved around me to hold our door open for me, and I blew him a teasing kiss, which he pretended to catch and hold dear, making me giggle. It wasn't long before I was back out of Tucker Hall and into the cold, taking the lighted path between my dorm and The Nic.

As I walked, happy, content, and otherwise completely relaxed, I started to notice some strange things. For the time of night it was, the shadows seemed to be getting longer, even closer to me. My footsteps seemed to echo a bit louder than I thought they should. A movement filled my peripheral vision, and in turning, I saw a wild and angry grin that I knew would fill my nightmares. That was the last thought I had before something hit my face and my world went black.

18

Owen

When ten minutes passed from Theo's text with no sign of him, I grew concerned. But when campus security pulled up not too far away with lights and sirens blazing, I knew something was wrong, and I took off from The Nic, not even caring that I didn't have my jacket on. I was off in a sprint and soon discovered a scene that made me sick to my stomach.

Two security officers were wrestling Aaron off into a squad car, where he was still screaming at the top of his lungs, "Fucking pussy freak! You had it coming! You had it coming!" I wanted to muzzle him myself, but my first concern was Theo, and I carefully kneeled by his side, reaching for my phone to text Brent and ask him to come out.

As I did so, Theo started to come to, trying to move and get up, and I put a hand lightly on his chest to limit his movements. "Did anyone get the number of that truck?"

I laughed, I couldn't help myself. Bloody and beaten, with a nose two times the size of Albuquerque, and his first reaction was to joke. "No, babe, but try not to move too much. You might have a concussion, or a spinal cord injury. We need to keep you as still as possible until the EMTs get here."

"What happened, Owen?"

"It looks like Aaron attacked you, babe." I hung my head slightly, feeling responsible. "I should have stayed with you, not let you walk alone. Maybe this wouldn't have happened."

"Hey." He reached his hand up to hold mine and squeezed it. "No blaming yourself." At least that's what he tried to say. His voice was so slurred it was much harder to understand. He tried to stare up at me with both eyes, but it was obvious it was too painful, and he let them close. "I do hurt though."

Brent chose that point to show up, handing me my jacket, which I quickly put on, and he went to work on evaluating Theo. "Theo, can you open those eyes for me briefly?" When he did so, Brent shined a flashlight into them and nodded before turning his attention to me and murmuring under his breath, "Definite concussion. Looking like a badly broken nose as well, thus all the blood."

"Bags? Off please."

I looked at Brent and he seemed to consider the situation. "You probably fell on your backpack, so you shouldn't be at risk for a spinal cord injury, but we're going to do this carefully anyway." As I watched, Brent started undoing the straps that held the backpack in place, and I followed his lead on the other side until the straps were hanging free. "Owen, I want you to hold Theo by the shoulders, steady as possible, while I slide the backpack out from underneath him. Then you're going to lower him to the ground."

Gripping Theo steadily by the shoulders, holding him off the ground, I let Brent slide the backpack away before I lowered Theo back down. "Where else do you hurt, babe?"

"My wrist and maybe my ribs too." I glanced off at the patrol car where Aaron was finally cordoned inside and gnashed my teeth, wanting to beat him with my own two hands for hurting Theo like this, but for the moment, I needed to focus on Theo and his needs.

Brent took to evaluating Theo's wrist, and it didn't take him long at all to share Theo's conclusion of a break. Carefully, he braced up the wrist, protecting it from further harm before giving Theo a bit of a sad look. "I've got nothing for your ribs, kiddo. I'm sorry. We're just going to have to wait out the EMTs and the painkillers they'll be able to give you."

"Okay," Theo whispered, and I sat beside his head, carefully running my fingers through his hair, trying to keep him as calm as possible.

One of the campus security officers came over to check on us, and realizing we had things at least as under control as we could, let us wait out the EMTs, which he promised were on their way. It was going to be a long ride to Susquehanna Regional Medical Center.

Brent went into his kit and cracked something open — it took me a moment to realize it was an ice pack. He placed a towel over the top part of Theo's face and then laid the ice pack on top, telling him, "That should help with some of the pain in your nose and face."

"Thank you," Theo told him softly, and I continued to run my fingers through his hair. "Owen?" I paused a second, waiting for his next words. "Hold my hand?" I scrambled into position, sitting beside Theo and holding his good hand, giving it a gentle squeeze and feeling him do the same in return. "I'm scared," he whispered.

"Don't be, babe. Brent and I are right here, and we're not going to let anything happen to you. When the EMTs come, I'll ride with them, so the only time I won't be with you in the next few hours is when they take you away for scans. But even then, I'll be in your room, waiting for you."

Brent assumed my position of sitting up near Theo's head, running fingers through his hair, and I shot him a grateful smile. Even though Theo startled a bit, Brent quieted him when he explained, "It's just me. Let us calm you down. It's going to be okay. We've got you basically ready to transport, and when they do take you, I'll take your bags up to our room for safekeeping." He paused, then went for the tease. "If I went through your stuff, what are the odds I'd find a cock ring?"

"Oh my Gawd. I'm never going to live that down, am I?" I whined, and even Theo managed a slight titter that didn't seem to cause him too much pain. "Tell a guy *one* secret about a cock ring, and you never hear the end of it."

"Three words," Theo started, "Brent and paddles." Brent went purple and I busted a gut laughing. But before we could get too giddy, Theo's voice went quiet again. "Guys? I'm kinda cold."

"Yep," Brent answered immediately and I watched him burrow in his kit, pulling out what I recognized as his emergency blanket. Settling it over Theo and tucking him in like a burrito, Brent asked, "Better?"

"Better," Theo agreed. His lips didn't look quite so blue, which was good, because I could finally hear sirens coming. But they weren't the ones I was expecting. The local police had responded to the scene, and they had many questions, not just for Theo, but for all of us.

"You say you have a previous history with the alleged perpetrator. When did it begin?"

"Couple of weeks into class," I offered. "Theo was getting harassed in the corner of the classroom by Aaron and two of his goons. Calling him a girl and telling him he didn't belong at this school. That was the norm for a while. Getting in his face and telling him he was a girl, inferior, and didn't belong."

The female officer snorted at that, but kept jotting down notes. "Has he escalated the situation before this point?" As I said, "no," Theo surprised me and said, "Yes."

The officer looked at him rather than me, and made a gesture for him to elaborate. Theo looked like he was really struggling to concentrate that hard, but he did it for the officers.

"A few things really. He tried to get us to break up at one point by implying I was a distraction to the lacrosse team, that no one liked me. Later, when that failed, and I was at a game, he let a ball whizz by my head. His most recent was definitely illegal, but I don't think this one," he pointed at me, "has reported it yet. But I've got all the evidence saved on my computer."

"Explain what you mean."

"It's a second degree misdemeanor. Unlawful Dissemination of Intimate Image. He posted images of Owen and a former girlfriend engaging in sexual activities on his FisherFriends feed. I saved copies of the images and screenshotted the page, showing where and when he'd posted it."

The officers exchanged looks before the female spoke again. "Any reason this wasn't reported earlier?"

I lowered my head slightly. "I tried to handle it myself. Let my coach resolve it. Y'see, Aaron is one of my teammates. I didn't want to cause a disruption on my team by causing trouble between him and me."

"How'd that work out for you?"

"As you can see by Theo's current condition? Not too well. This is my fault."

"Babe..." Theo interrupted, but I interrupted him back.

"No. I should have just manned up and went to the deans much earlier. It would have not only saved us heartache, but your injuries. I'm supposed to protect you, and I dropped the fucking ball."

"Though we've got all of our information, we're going to stay with you guys until the ambulance shows up, which should be shortly. You warm enough, young man? We've got more blankets if you need them."

"I'm okay," Theo whispered, and his lips no longer looked blue, but I still gestured towards the officer to grab another blanket, and one went off to do so. The officer laid the additional blanket over top of Theo and he shifted just slightly, wincing before making a happy noise. "That feels nice."

"Ribs bothering you?" I asked.

"Yeah," Theo murmured in response. About that time, another set of sirens approached, and this time they were for the ambulance. When they arrived, Brent talked with the EMTs over his observations while the other EMT carefully tugged Theo's arm from beneath the blanket to check his blood pressure. Apparently satisfied, he tucked Theo back into his burrito and went to get the stretcher, bringing it to Theo's side.

"Okay, Theo. Just to be on the safe side, we're going to put you in a c-collar and then on the backboard. So, Officer, Owen, can you help tip him in your direction while we slide it underneath him?" We obliged, and I could hear Theo whimper, no doubt from rib pain, before we lowered him back down onto the backboard. They secured his head in place, removing the ice pack from his face. "You're doing great, Theo, just hang in there for us."

When the EMT counted to four, we all lifted Theo onto the stretcher, and I moved to follow, fully intending to go to the hospital with him. "Brent, can you take the bags and put them in our room? He'll probably need clean clothes for when they release him, though, and we'll need a ride."

"I've got you," my roommate promised, and in that moment I wanted to hug him. Instead I climbed up inside the ambulance, getting out of the EMTs way, but trying to hold Theo's hand.

"How far is this hospital from here?"

"About forty-five minutes," the driving EMT answered, and Theo groaned softly.

"Could I have some painkillers then? Not enough to make me pass out, I know you're worried about a concussion, but enough to dull the pain in my ribs?"

"Sure," answered the more cheerful of the EMTs, and after warning Theo about feeling a slight pinch, they were running a line for fluids and painkillers. The painkillers seemed to have their desired effect and the strain on Theo's face disappeared, replaced by a more relaxed expression.

The ride was otherwise uneventful; no lights and sirens since Theo wasn't critical, and not a lot of conversation between Theo and his happy-go-lucky EMT in the back with us. I remained out of the way, just holding his hand, trying to reassure him with my presence. Sometimes he seemed especially scared and clung tighter, but for the most part, Theo was handling things like a champ.

When we arrived at the hospital, the EMTs told him they were going to get him into a room so they could do their initial scans and assess the full extent of his damage. I followed the stretcher to the room they'd set up for him, plopping down in a chair beside Theo's good hand and grabbing it once they'd got him off the stretcher and onto the bed.

It didn't take long for a nurse to come in to take his vitals and to run over the chart the EMTs had left behind. "Okay, Theo. I see you'll be needing a CAT scan and a few X-rays, and then we'll be rolling you up to a room for the night for observation, since it's so late in the evening."

"Okay," Theo agreed.

"Will I be able to stay with him?" I asked, and the nurse gave me a soft smile.

"Unlimited time while he's in here and technically only an hour once he's in his room, but if you bypass the nurses' station when they bring him up, then they won't be able to tell how long you've been in there." She winked at me and I managed a grin, nodding my head at her.

An orderly came in at that point and said, "Let's get you off to X-ray, young man." He glanced my way and smiled. "We'll be back soon."

I nodded, and it really wasn't too long before Theo was back again — then leaving once more for his CAT scan. Finally they were returning him, and the same original nurse looked at me and told me, "I'm bringing him upstairs, Owen. Hang on my coattails, and we'll do a Mission: Impossible entrance."

I laughed, and even Theo gave a few giggles, and we maneuvered our way up two floors, where Theo was settled into a room of his own. "So what did they tell you, babe?" I asked once he was comfortably in his hospital bed, covered up with blankets and relaxing.

"Broken wrist, but a clean fracture, so it'll heal on its own with only a cast as intervention. Broken ribs, but there's nothing much they can do there. Concussion, but a relatively mild one, which is why I'm not nauseous or seeing double or anything. No bleeding in my brain or in my chest cavity."

"Good." I relaxed, not even realizing how much I'd been worrying about all that, and took his hand again, staring at him for the longest time before it all kind of hit me and I lowered my head to his lap and started to cry.

"Oh, Owen, what's wrong, love?"

"I could have lost you tonight," I said between sniffles. "I could have lost you and you wouldn't have known that I loved you too."

I think I was almost as shocked as he was that the words came out, but Theo stilled, then squeezed my hand, assuring me softly, "I'm still here. For keeps, remember?"

Still more than a bit choked up, I kept my face buried and whispered to him, "I'm quitting the lacrosse team. I think Brent will follow."

"What? Why?"

"Because they're not really any sort of family when they watch one of their extended family get harassed to the point of physical abuse and do nothing. They were a family of convenience, and I understand that now. You and Brent are my family, and I love you both, but very differently."

"Oh, Owen, you love lacrosse."

"I love you more," I told him resolutely. "I know the school will start an investigation at some point into what happened to you. When they do, I'm going to tell them about telling the coach — twice — about the harassment and the pictures, and him not doing anything worth note."

"The school has a zero tolerance policy," Theo noted. "He probably violated it in trying to protect his prized player."

"He may lose his job," I agreed, "and I wouldn't object if they disbanded the whole team. Brent made me see how toxic it is, how the underlying environment and culture is one of intolerance. No matter how good the sport might be for my resume, the experience isn't good for my heart and soul."

Theo carefully tilted his head, as though trying not to rattle it further. "Maybe we both could spend more time with Pride Council? I like getting to know the guys. Like Beau? I just want to give him a big hug all the time."

"Yeah, I know what you mean. You wouldn't think a kid coming from money would have it so miserable, but..." I shook my head. "He definitely needs us. And thankfully his found family is a lot more supportive than mine was."

Who knows what we'd have continued talking about, but our conversation was loudly interrupted by two adults that resembled Theo — his parents? But how did they get here that fast?

19

Theo

When my parents burst into my hospital room, the only thing I could do was groan and cling tighter to Owen's hand with my good one. They took us in, exchanged looks, and then my dad spoke in a tone that brokered no arguments. "When they release you, we're taking you home and suing this school."

"No. You're not." My parents gaped at me, and Owen lowered his head just enough so they couldn't see he was biting on his lip not to chuckle at me. "I'm nineteen, almost twenty years old. The royalty money is in my name and is legally mine, and if this is where I want to go to school, this is where I'm going to go to school."

My dad folded his arms across his chest, looking like he was preparing for an argument, but I just stared back at him in a silent challenge. After a moment, he wilted and came to me, wrapping his arms around my shoulders. "God, son, we were so worried; we caught the first flight we could and then drove the rest."

"I know that worried feeling quite well." Owen had risen to his feet, his full moose height, and reached out to shake my father's hand. "I'm Owen. Owen Lewis. Your son's boyfriend."

"Pleased to meet you, just not under these circumstances," Dad answered, and after a firm shake, he and Mom sat on the other side of my bed, eying my broken wrist. "The police told us you were here, and why, but nothing further. What are your injuries?"

"Broken wrist — clean, will just require a few weeks of casting. Broken nose, it'll heal on its own. Broken ribs, time will heal them, too. Concussion, they're observing me overnight, but it's not a big concern. There was no bleeding in my brain or my abdomen. Considering I was caught completely off-guard and weighed down by bags, I think I was rather lucky."

"Weighed down by bags?" my mom asked.

"Yeah, I was getting ready to spend the weekend in Owen's dorm," I answered, not the least bit surprised when my parents exchanged looks.

"How old are you, Owen?"

"Why does it matter?" I growled. "He's twenty-one, he's a junior, and he works his ass off in the bookstore."

Owen squeezed my good hand gently. "He forgot the part about where I love your son. Personally, I find him one of the most beautiful people I've ever met."

Mom swooned a little bit, but Dad remained stoic. "The police mentioned this wasn't a one-time incident. Have you young men been reporting these actions to the school for them to address?"

I looked at Owen, and though he bit his lip, he addressed my father's concerns. "No, sir. We were trying to deal with it on our own. You see, Aaron, the assailant, was one of my lacrosse teammates, and I was trying to avoid causing mayhem on my team by going to the deans. In hindsight, that was a very big mistake, one that I regret dearly."

"So you pressured Theo not to report this clown?"

"Dad!" I protested, but Owen held up a hand and spoke again.

"I didn't pressure him, but I did request time. And as I said, that was my mistake. I didn't realize Aaron was that bent and was capable of what he did tonight. If I had, I never would have left Theo alone, because there's no way he would have tried to attack him had I been there."

"You let him walk alone?!?"

"Yes, Dad. I'm a big boy. I'm capable of walking alone, along lighted paths, between two dorms. I don't need a babysitter. I have a boyfriend, but that's what I prefer." Owen leaned over to kiss my forehead, and Mom definitely swooned at that, but still, she remained quiet.

Dad didn't seem to know what to say to me, so he turned to Owen instead. "You love my son."

"I do, very much," Owen told him. "In fact, before you two came in here I was thinking about how I could convince the school to let me move into a senior apartment early and have Theo there with me. They'd have to bypass their rule on frosh being in frosh dorms, but I think given the situation, they might consider it."

Dad tilted his head. "Do you think it would help if I pushed for it?" He paused, then looked in my direction. "Assuming that's what you want of course."

I smiled wide. "No, Dad, I'd hate to live with my boyfriend for the remainder of the semester and next year. Please don't make that happen." When he rolled his eyes, I laughed, and even Mom did too, and I winked over at Owen.

"I think the school will be willing to work with us to avoid a lawsuit. Because even if you two didn't report things, they should have been aware of the possibility of extra harassment for you and been on the lookout for it."

"I'm kinda glad they didn't treat me differently, to be honest," I told them softly. "Excluding the issues caused by Aaron, I've gotten a real college experience, from running to the doughnut shop at the crack of dawn to falling asleep in my boyfriend's arms at night."

Owen squeezed my hand again and I smiled at him, mouthing to him, "your arms feel like home," and I swear I thought he was going to tear up again. My hand got squeezed a little bit harder, and Owen stayed focused on me completely. As we sat there, I had a thought, and I turned to first my parents and then Owen.

"Did anyone think to call Harv and let him know what's going on?"

Owen shook his head. "I don't believe so, but I can text Brent and ask him to give Harv a call. That way if he *did* hear about the attack, he won't be worried. Though to be honest, had he heard, I'd be expecting him to be blowing up your phone."

"He could be," I admitted. "My phone was in my backpack."

"That would explain why you didn't answer our calls," my mother said, and I gave her a small shrug as if to say "oops." "Though to be fair, we figured you were indisposed, so it wasn't *too* much of a concern. That the police had let us know you were awake and alert before you took the ambulance ride helped."

I turned my attention to Owen. "Get in touch with Brent please?" I rifled off Harv's number to him and then leaned back against the thin stack of pillows, sighing softly. "Did they say if I could sleep yet?"

"They'll wake you every few hours," my dad said, and I sighed harder. "You seem to have things under control here, so I think your mom and I are going to find a nearby hotel and then go to the school in the morning to have a talk with the deans about your situation. Don't worry, we won't threaten them *too* much."

I groaned, but I did appreciate that my parents were going to fight for me to be able to stay with Owen on a more permanent basis. I accepted hugs from both parents, and soon, they were on their way. It wasn't but a matter of minutes after they'd left that a nurse arrived to do vitals, and I asked her, "Any idea when I might get released?"

"I know they want to cast your wrist in the morning, so I'd imagine after that point. You don't really have any extenuating circumstances keeping you here. Even keeping you here overnight now is exercising an abundance of caution. You look good, beyond your ribs and your nose, you probably feel pretty good, and we can send you back to campus with painkillers to help counter what you *are* feeling."

I sighed with relief and looked over at Owen. "How much longer are you going to stay here?"

"As long as they'll let me. I'd stay overnight if I could."

The nurse must have thought we were adorable or something because she had an "awww" look on her face. "Unfortunately you can't stay overnight. In fact, visiting hours were already over when you two got here, but everyone has turned a blind eye to your presence. You don't want to push your luck, though."

Owen sighed, and I nodded my understanding. "Call Brent, ask him to pick you up?" I asked, knowing Owen was without a vehicle.

"Yeah. That'll be at least forty-five minutes though. Can I at least hang out here until that point?"

The nurse nodded. "I'll let the rest of the crew know you're just waiting for your ride. And in the meantime, Theo, we'll try and keep you as comfortable as possible. If you'd like a painkiller at this point, you'll need to ask for it."

I interrupted her to say, "Please."

She nodded again. "I'll call that in for you. Recognize you're not going to get much rest tonight, simply because of the nature of your head injury and the fact that you're in a hospital. I'm not the doctor, but I would suggest resting for a few days when you get back on campus. I'm sure the doctor will provide a note to get you out of classes."

"Some of my classes I can do online sessions of, so there's that."

She gave me a thumbs up. "Sit tight. I'll be back with the painkiller."

Once she left, Owen looked me over, asking softly, "Besides asking for painkillers, how are you feeling?"

"I'm...okay? My ribs and face are throbbing, but I'm not in agony by any stretch. It certainly could be worse, and I'm grateful for..." I paused, then furrowed my brow, realizing I didn't quite know how the situation had ended.

Seeming to realize that, Owen explained. "Campus security nabbed Aaron. I'd guess you were within The Nic's camera range when Aaron got you, and they came. I got worried when you weren't there within ten minutes and ran outside, and I found you on the ground with them trying to corral Aaron. You were just coming around when I reached you."

"So I was out for a few minutes, it sounds like. Probably for the best I don't remember the attack at all. I'm sure I'll have nightmares about this anyway, but they'd be worse if I could see his face during the attack."

The nurse came back in with two pills and poured me water from my jug. Handing me the small cup and pills, I was able to toss them back and swallow down the water, shivering as the cold hit my throat. The nurse smiled at me then went on her way, leaving me alone with Owen again.

Looking at him, I gave him a wry smile. "I had a teacher in high school who was big on the Victorian era. Taught us slang. And there's one line in particular that's quite apt and will make you laugh out loud."

"Oh?"

"Indeed. I'm not up to dick."

Owen didn't laugh, but he did smirk, dark eyes twinkling devilishly. "So you're telling me I've got to keep it in my pants for now. I suppose I can *handle* that." Finally Owen started laughing, and I joined in, even though it hurt my ribs to do so. After a moment, Owen glanced at his phone and then back at me. "Brent is bringing you some of your clothes. Night clothes for tonight. Clean clothes for tomorrow. Says he hopes you don't mind that he went through your bags."

"I'm surprised he didn't comment on the toy selection," I deadpanned, and Owen's eyes widened.

"Did you really bring the cock ring?" he asked in a low whisper, and I started laughing again, even though it left me clutching my ribs.

"I might have. But it was in a little velvet bag, so unless he got *really* curious, he wouldn't have found it. Seriously though, if Brent gets too feisty, just buy one of those toy plastic paddles, and tell him to go entertain himself with Misha. He'll go purple and shut right up."

This time it was Owen's turn to giggle, even though he looked embarrassed by the whole discussion.

"You're too much," I teased. "You can talk about your dick and my dick and all the things you're going to do to me, but I start talking about Brent's paddle and you get red-faced."

"Because it's Brent's! I don't want to know about him and a paddle or what he and Misha do with it!"

"Come here," I instructed him, and when he came closer, I stretched my good arm up and hooked it around his neck, tugging him in for a soft kiss. "I love you," I whispered against his lips, and he smiled lightly. "I know this is hard for you, seeing me like this, but please believe me when I tell you that I'm okay, that I'm going to remain okay, and that we'll get through this."

"Alright," Owen agreed as he lightly pressed a kiss against my forehead. "I don't know how we're going to get you back to school yet. We may have to coordinate that with your parents."

"Yeah, they can probably take me back, especially if they have a hotel near here. That makes more sense than making Brent waste gas to drive up here again. I mean I know he'd do it without complaint, but it's not fair to him."

Owen nodded. "He'd definitely do that for you. I wouldn't go so far as to say he loves you too, but he does me, and he certainly appreciates that you love me as well."

I quirked a smile that deepened wider when a nurse arrived with Brent in tow. "Glad to see you looking better, Theo."

"Thank you for looking after me, Brent. And for everything you did and continue to do. It's appreciated more than you know."

He smiled back at me. "It's what friends are for, yeah?" He came in closer, setting a paper bag on the bed. "Clothes. Night stuff and clothes for tomorrow. Want us to take what you were wearing in the ER so we can see about washing it?"

I gave him a sad smile. "I feel like it's my jacket that took the brunt of the blood, and that might not be cleanable. I can afford a new parka if it comes down to it, but it might be better to bring it back and then let my mom have a go at trying to clean it."

"Good plan," Brent agreed as he went around the bed to retrieve the dirty clothes. He reached for my good hand and gave it a squeeze before he went back to where the nurse was waiting, looking at Owen expectantly. "Go on, suck face so we can get back to campus before the werewolves come out to play."

I giggled at Brent and Owen flushed, but he did lean closer to give me another gentle kiss, whispering to me, "I love you. I'll see you tomorrow. Sweet dreams, okay?"

"I'll do my best," I promised. I waited until they were out of the room to carefully climb from the bed, holding onto the rail an extra moment to ensure I was steady. Then I dug through the bag to find my nightclothes, swooning a little bit with the realization that Brent had sent along one of Owen's T-shirts for me to sleep in. Getting out of the johnny didn't take long, nor did climbing into the sleep clothes, and I was infinitely more comfortable.

Alone and left to my own devices, I turned the TV on in my room, finding a hockey game and settling on that. I wasn't sure who was playing or what the score was, but the game itself appeared exciting, and that was all I needed. I rested my head back against the pillow and just tried to get some sleep while I could.

The next thing I was aware of was someone shaking me awake, calling my name. "Theo. Theo! THEO!" I finally blinked my eyes open, bringing my good arm up to rub the sleep from bleary eyes and gaze in the direction of what I now realized was a nurse. "You were having a nightmare," she told me. "You were terrified, screaming. Several neighboring patients called in to the nurses station to alert us to your situation." She paused for a moment, then asked, "Would you like me to bring a therapist in, to talk with you about what happened?"

Biting my lip lightly, I finally nodded, telling her, "I don't know exactly what happened though. And I'm not sure if what my mind is creating is better or worse than what actually occurred."

She rubbed my shoulder lightly, soothingly, and then told me, "Let me see who I can find available at this hour, and as soon as I've got someone, I'll send them up to you. Try to stay awake if you can."

I snorted — that would be easier said than done given how tired I was. But after adjusting the bed to a more upright position, I carefully pushed myself up higher as well, asking the nurse just before she hit the door, "Would a cup of coffee be possible?"

"I'll see what I can do for you," she promised, and then she was out the door.

I dragged my good hand down my face and sighed. So much for thinking I was handling things well. I guess I should have known better than to think this wouldn't affect me, that Aaron could attack me and the only scars would be physical.

20

Owen

It was a whole new world for Brent and me, now that we had finished moving into the senior apartments here on campus. Theo's parents had instilled enough fear into the Roseden authorities that they readily agreed to let me move with the understanding that Theo would be joining me. And he had, curled up in my very first private bedroom of my life.

In between classes for the day, I ducked my head into the room to check on him. "Do you need anything, babe?"

Theo gave me a tired smile. "No, I'm okay. I've got the coffee Brent made earlier, and I can always get up and brew more. I'm not a total invalid, y'know."

And while that may have been true, I was still worried about that nagging rib injury and the pain it continued to cause him. Theo wasn't big on taking the painkillers, which I totally got, but sometimes I thought he'd benefit more from them than he was allowing himself to. "I know you're not," I finally said gently. "I just worry about you. I do love you, remember."

A grin lit up his face. "I'll never get tired of hearing you say that. Even if I had to scare you half to death to get those words out of you."

"To be fair, it wasn't you scaring me, it was Mr. I've Been Expelled From School." That news had just come down in the last few hours — Aaron had been expelled for not only assaulting another classmate, but violating the school's code of conduct. We fully expected his parents to put up a huge stink about the whole mess, but they didn't really have a leg to stand on. Besides his assault charge, Aaron had also been hit with the unlawful intimate photo charge, thanks to Theo saving the photos and screenshots from my FisherFriends timeline.

The grin was replaced with a grimace. "Let's not talk about him anymore. It's bad enough I keep seeing his face in nightmares." Those nightmares, while not as severe as his episode in the hospital had apparently been, were enough that he was waking us both up at night. I could usually feel his anxiety ramping up, but I couldn't yet pull him from the nightmares before they occurred.

"Are you going to go visit the therapist today?" I asked, because he'd seen her several times already in the week or so since he'd been released from the hospital, and I couldn't keep track of their schedule.

"I'm not scheduled to, but if I need to, I could send her an email. I mean, we know what my general root issue is, it's just convincing my mind to chill out about it all."

"It's not that simple and you know it," I chided, "or I wouldn't be finally seeing a school therapist too, at your suggestion I might remind you." I'd only been once, but that session had opened up a bottleneck of emotion that I'd kept trapped for a long time. Feelings about being loved, being abandoned, and just being wanted in general. And while Theo did a good job soothing my wounded inner child now, he still wept for my past pain.

Theo looked embarrassed. "I wasn't trying to mock the sessions, I swear it to you. I just feel like my situation should be easier to resolve than yours. This was a one time deal..."

"It wasn't," I interrupted. "You've been dealing with him since your arrival here this semester. It built over time, and no doubt built up your anxieties along with it. The attack may have been the tipping point, but it wasn't like it was out of the blue."

He looked like he was going to argue, but after a moment he just sighed and nodded. "You're right; I know you're right. I just hate this. I hate feeling weak, and it's bad enough I'm injured. The mental duress just seems to make it worse."

I came further into the room until I was sitting on the edge of the bed, realizing I was probably going to miss my next class but not caring. Cupping his face with my hand, I told him softly, "You're not weak. That asshole was bonkers, and *he* is going to need therapy to figure out what's wrong with him. Assuming his parents would ever allow such a thought, that there might be something *wrong* with their silver-spooned baby."

"I still think he's gay and deeply repressed."

Leaning to kiss Theo's forehead, I shrugged. "Could be. But beyond erasing him from your nightmares, he doesn't matter anymore. We can feel empathy for him, but he brought his situation on himself."

Theo nodded and reached for my free hand, trying to tug me into the bed with him. I smiled, and after taking a step back to shed my backpack, I joined him in the big bed, letting my lips linger against his for a soft kiss.

"I love you," I breathed to him, and he lit up like a starry filled night, positively glowing, and it made me joyous to be able to have that effect on him. "I think they're deciding on Coach's fate today."

"Yeah? Do you think he stands a chance of keeping his job?"

"Knowing what I do now?" I shook my head. "It's bad enough that he treated my concerns as 'boys will be boys,' but that he specifically ignored the zero tolerance policy in place for escalating those types of concerns is damning. And I've heard rumblings that the team will be disbanded, as well, that they think the culture in the locker room is too toxic to safely field a team for the rest of the season. Which, from a purely athletic standpoint, is a shame. They had a good record."

"But they weren't good people," Theo countered, and I nodded, because he was right.

"Maybe I should have realized that when no one was really outright accepting of my relationship with you. It's not like they treated me differently, but..."

"I get what you're saying. It would have been nice if someone had come up to you and said they had your back. Or that they respected your right to be happy. Anything to let you know that they cared."

"Right. Like, Brent would get asked how Misha was, or about her classes and stuff like that. No one ever asked me about you." I turned away from Theo for a moment, feeling the emotional impact of that rejection hit me. "They were supposed to be my family," I cried out mournfully.

"Oh, babe." Theo tugged me towards him so that my head ended up on his shoulder, and I buried my face against his neck, hot tears burning a path along his skin. "Let it out, love. I've got you." And so I cried. I cried for the loss of what had been my family, for the time wasted giving them priority over Theo, and for just being so foolish in general.

I'm not even sure how long I was crying, but when I finally managed to get a grip on myself, I was hiccuping and my nose was running. Theo reached to get me a tissue, and I blew my nose loudly, the sound resembling a foghorn. Taking a deep breath, I steeled myself and sat up, looking at Theo with still wet eyes. "Thank you."

"You don't ever have to thank me for being there for you." His chastisement was gentle but on point. "For keeps, remember?"

"For keeps," I echoed.

Theo turned his head to nuzzle me and I chased another kiss, this one a little more passionate than the last. Hot, open-mouthed kisses littered our faces, while tongues tangled frequently for dominance. No one got me as hot as Theo did, but I was going to have to keep my "little friend" in check because his rib injury wouldn't allow for messing around.

Between kisses, I said, "Dinner," and Theo pulled back to start laughing at me.

"Think with your stomach, much?" he teased, and I flipped him the bird. "I was thinking we should try out the kitchenette. We've got food, right?"

I bit on my lower lip. "Maybe? If Brent went out, then *he* has food, and I'm sure he'd share, but we should contribute if that is the case. If he could drive us, we could always pick up food ourselves." And even though I liked the idea of being somewhat self-sufficient, I inwardly cringed at spending money.

"What's wrong?" he asked, running fingertips along my arm, making me shiver just a little bit.

"My consummate concern. Money. I'm not going to need a car this summer in Mystic because of the housing they're providing me with, but I will need a car by the time I graduate. And a car is never just a car. It's gas, insurance, and an emergency fund for random repairs." I sighed, feeling myself getting worked up again.

"*Cálmate*," Theo instructed, and I managed a chuckle at him of all people telling me to calm down in Spanish. "Better. Remember you're going to be making decent money at the Seaport since it's a paid internship. Plus you're not paying for housing. You'll just be buying food for yourself, and I'll chip in when I come to visit. Which I'll try to make as many weekends as possible."

I smiled a bit more at the thought of Theo coming to visit me in Mystic. I was well aware that my Research Assistant position had the chance to become something more after graduation, and the opportunity to work for one of the preeminent maritime research institutes in the country had me salivating. Plus, Connecticut would put me closer to Theo's family, and we'd gotten on well while they were in town getting the school straightened out.

"Do you want to go to the cafeteria and see what they've got tonight, and then when Brent gets back, we can talk to him about grocery shopping and splitting the bill three ways?" I started to protest to 'three ways,' but Theo was having no part of it. "No, I live here too. It's only fair that I contribute. I'd feel the same way if Misha was living here."

"That sounds like a good idea." Carefully, I climbed over the top of Theo and off the bed, reaching out my hands to help him rise to a standing position. Looking him up and down, I drooled a little bit — his boxers defined him in all the right places, from the curves of his ass cheeks to the developing muscles in his legs. "You're gorgeous, have I told you that lately?"

Blushing fiercely, Theo moved past me to go into the closet we were sharing, pulling out sweats and a Roseden hoodie. Sadly, we'd retired most of my lacrosse clothing after I'd quit the team, but I was determined to get more clothes to "share" with Theo. Once he had his clothes on, I nudged him towards my desk chair so that I could put his sneakers on him. He probably could have done it on his own, but bending over was still uncomfortable for him, so it was easier for me to do his shoes instead.

"I think it's fried chicken and mac and cheese today," I told him, "which works for me, since I'm not strictly watching my diet anymore."

"Tasty," Theo agreed. "Are you for dessert?"

I coughed and choked, staring at him wide-eyed as he laughed at me. "Me? No! Your ribs couldn't handle that, you dork."

He batted his eyelashes at me. "My ribs wouldn't be involved if I was jerking you off and then licking my hand clean." I groaned as his words had an immediate impact on me that he picked up on. He grabbed a hold of my dick through my jeans and gave it a squeeze, making me whine in frustration. "You know you want me."

"Fuck! Fine. So long as you know that turnabout is fair play once you're feeling better." I tried to give him a dirty look, but he was too busy smirking at me to notice or care, and I finally just huffed out my protest.

"I'm sure you'll be making me scream for all the right reasons, babe." Theo gave me a cheeky little grin and grabbed for my hand, using it to pull himself back to his feet. "C'mon, let's get some grub."

The walk from the senior apartments to the cafeteria was a bit longer than it had been from the dorms, and for that reason I kept a close eye on Theo. He'd been cleared for walking short distances, and I wasn't quite sure this qualified, but he didn't appear to be laboring too much. Then again, I'm not sure he'd allow his pain to show, either.

Once we finally arrived and scanned our meal cards in, Theo shot me another grin. "Looks like you were right. Fried chicken and mac and cheese. You'll find a wheelbarrow and roll me out of here if it comes down to it, right?"

I snorted at him. "As if. You'll be needing to roll me, buster."

Theo was still laughing when we picked up our food and found a table to sit at opposite each other. Rather than dig right into my food, I stretched a hand across the table and let my fingers dance over top of his hand, seeing him smile as I did so. "Shouldn't you be eating?" he teased.

I promptly used my free hand to bring a piece of fried chicken up to my mouth and took a bite, chomping and chewing and then winking at him, all the while continuing to touch him.

"Touché." Instead of going for the chicken, Theo dug into the mac and cheese with a gusto, complete with little decadent moans of pleasure.

"You're horrible," I complained, but not really. "You don't even enjoy yourself this much when we're having sex." I grinned at him to show I didn't mean it, and his eyes danced in my direction.

"Well, we haven't actually had *sex* yet, so you've got nothing to compare it to. Lots of oral and hand jobs and rutting, but no penetration."

"Truuuuuuuuuuuuuuue," I dragged out. "We'll need to rectify that at some point." I glanced around to make sure no one was exceptionally close and able to overhear our conversation. "You *do* have a strap-on and supplies for it now, yes?"

"If you're asking if I'm ready and willing to own your ass, the answer is a resounding yes. Just let my ribs heal and I'll pound you into oblivion."

How he managed to completely kill me with a straight face, I'd never quite figure out, but I was so hard I could have used my cock as a hammer to put nails in. I'm sure my eyes were darker than normal, and the cheeky shit's only reaction to that was to snicker.

"Just you wait," I warned him. "I will make you scream so many times in a row, make you so weak in the knees, that you won't be able to walk for a week."

"Please?"

"You're incorrigible," I told him, but I was laughing, too.

We took our time eating, with me continuing to touch him the entire time, be it with my hand or a foot sliding up his leg. There could be no doubt — I loved him, I wanted him, I desired him.

By the time we made it back to the apartments, however, Theo looked a bit worse for wear. "Too much walking?" I chided, and though he shot me a dirty look, he didn't argue. "C'mon, let's get you back to bed." He was leaning against me by the time we reached our room, and I helped him strip out of his shoes and then his sweats.

"We were supposed to talk to Brent," he offered as a minor protest.

"It can wait," I told him firmly. I eased him into the bed, then set about stripping myself, getting down to my boxer briefs but putting a pair of sweats back on to add a layer of clothing between us and avoid sneaky fingers trying to put a move on me.

"This sucks."

"I know, love, but remember what the doctor said. You need rest. That's why the school is letting you take your classes online for the time being." I climbed over to lay next to him, and I leaned up to kiss along his neck, feeling him melt at the touches. "That's it," I breathed. "Just relax."

Theo sank into the cushioned pillow top of my mattress, all but turning into a pile of goo at my loving affections. I let my nose move along his ear and he sighed happily, making me smile to myself. Perhaps I'd be able to persuade him to fall asleep, get some of that rest he so desperately needed. "I wish I could curl up on you," he whispered, and I brought a hand up to stroke his cheek.

"I know, babe. Soon though. Just think about that. Soon," I promised, and though this sigh of his wasn't nearly as happy, at least he wasn't grumbling. I continued to keep my hands on him, lightly touching him, just fleeting affectionate touches to remind him that I was there and that I loved him.

Soon, he relaxed even further, his bodyweight sagging bonelessly as sleep started to pull him away from me. I wouldn't always be able to watch him as he slept and prevent nightmares, but for now, I could.

I promised to protect him, and protect him I would.

21

Theo

It was spring break time, and while most of the campus had gone to parts warmer — or just home — for the two weeks, Owen and I stayed on campus. He'd picked up extra shifts at the bookstore, increasing his savings and safety net, which was one of those things I understood he needed the most.

I'd finally been cleared for exercise again just before spring break started, and Brent and I had resumed running. It amazed me how good that felt, though that first run was a bit nauseating after so much time away.

Today, I walked campus, enjoying the warmer weather and the general quiet from the lack of people. Though there was one person I knew was still on campus — Harv. My roommate had told me he'd be sticking around, because he didn't want to deal with his parents, the illustrious Dr. and Mrs. Patrick Caleb Bates. Given the stories he'd told me about his family, his upbringing, and even his unique name, I couldn't blame him for staying at school.

I let myself into Tucker Hall and then jogged up the stairs to my old room, opening the door and calling out before I was fully inside. "Hey, Harv! Miss me?"

But it was clear by the very red face of him and his companion that he hadn't missed me that much at all. Harv's hair was sticking up at several angles, his pupils were blown, and if my eyes weren't deceiving me, he was very kissed up indeed.

His companion still had a grip on Harv's collar, and I teasingly called out, "Unhand him, you knave!" Harv was unceremoniously dropped for his troubles, still landing on his feet, and the companion looked like he was going to make a run for the exit, but I stopped him. "Wait! You can't leave until I've interrogated you."

"Theeeeeeeo," Harv whined, and while he was embarrassed, I was still more than a bit shocked to have caught him in our room making out with a *man*. So much for the swimsuit model calendar!

"Hi! I'm Theo," I introduced myself to the redhead still looking to make an escape. He had pretty green eyes that almost reminded me of cat eyes, but Owen was still prettier to me. "And you are?"

"Ian. Ian Winter." He shook my offered hand, and after making a resigned sigh, moved to sit on what had been my bunk. "Go on, give me your worst."

I gave him an easy smile. "Nah, just curious how long the two of you have been pulling the wool over my eyes. Harv, you had me fooled!"

My friend quirked a smile at me. "I know. You thought I was straight. I didn't see a need to correct you until a situation called for that to change. I'm actually pansexual, and, well, Ian here is good justification for me telling you that. So I was never really joining Pride Council to be an ally; I was joining for myself."

"As for how long we've been seeing each other?" Ian offered. "This is pretty new. Less than a month. He started tutoring me in English Lit and it just went from there."

"Young love. Awwww!" I teased, and Harv made no qualms about flipping me off. I returned the favor, and the next thing, a pillow was flying my way. "Shit!" I was being bombarded with throw pillows — even Ian was in on the action. "I surrender!"

Harv cackled before I unburied myself from pillows, peeking out to find him and Ian exchanging an affectionate glance. It was truly adorable, and it made me very happy to see Harv had found someone to make him as happy as Owen made me.

"I honestly didn't mean to interrupt you guys," I told them as I tossed a throw in Ian's direction, which he easily caught and put back on the bed. "I just hadn't seen you in awhile, Harv, and knowing you were here this week, and with Owen working extra hours, I figured I'd stop by."

Harv's eyes danced. "My fault, really. I knew Ian was going to be around, too, and I should have warned you. Or gotten you a bell so I could have heard you coming."

"Oh trust me, you'd hear me coming," I said playfully, and though he went bright red, Harv was laughing just as hard as I was.

"And to think we once had to work on your confidence. My God. Ian, I'm glad you're getting to meet this variation of Theo, because he's entertaining to be around."

"I see that!" Ian came off the bed to grab a few more of the pillows at my feet and settle them on the bed, his eyes no longer showing fear or wariness and instead alight with happiness. "I know this was your room and all, Theo, but would you mind if I kick you out? I'd like to get back to getting it on with your roommate."

I laughed so hard I snorted, making them both laugh at me. "Can't say I've been kicked out of my own room before, but I'm totally agreeable. Ian, leave him a hickey or two. I need something to pick on him about the next time I visit. And, Harv? Maybe I'll even wear a bell for you..."

With that thought — and their laughter — ringing in my ears, I left the room, hearing a low growl just before the door snicked shut. Incorrigible. But endearing as fuck.

Once I was out of Tucker Hall, I glanced at my watch, noting that noon was quickly approaching. It stood to reason that Owen hadn't thought to grab lunch before he left for work earlier, since he was normally out of the bookstore by now, so I decided to stop at the campus sandwich shop to pick him up his favorite steak and cheese.

It didn't take me long to get the sandwich, with extra peppers because I loved my man, or make the short walk over to the bookstore. I was greeted with a "Hey, sexy," when I came through the door, and I playfully shook his sandwich at him.

"You better not be greeting all of your customers that way."

"Nah, just the sexy ones," Owen deadpanned, and I narrowed my eyes but couldn't stop the grin, completely defeating the purpose. "Grabbed yourself a sandwich? I wish I had thought to do that."

"You didn't have to. I thought of it for you." Owen gaped at me then bounced over to practically tackle hug me.

"Ahhhhh! Thank you! I wasn't sure what I was going to do for lunch."

"Lock up and let's go sit for a bit while you eat," I suggested, and Owen did just that, locking up the bookshop, putting the back in thirty minutes sign up, and grabbing my hand to tug me off to The Big Dough to sit and eat.

When we arrived, we were surprised to find we weren't the only ones there. Beau Thernstrom was at the counter, staring blankly into the distance, with his boyfriend, Damian Leonhardt, nowhere to be seen. "How now, brown cow?" I asked, nudging him on our way past.

Beau shook himself out of his daze, then turned in our direction as we settled in at a nearby table. "Fighting with Damian. Supposed to be staying at Coach's house during break, but it feels awkward when I'm not on speaking terms with his son."

"Do you want to talk about it?" Owen questioned gently, indicating the open seat at our table, and after a long hesitation, Beau came over and joined us.

Turning his chair backwards and leaning against the top, Beau's voice was sad when he spoke. "I don't even know how it got this far. We were fighting over stupid shit and it just escalated and escalated until we weren't talking at all and he went back to New Jersey for spring break instead of staying with his pops."

"So you're stuck at campus, heart in your throat, and not wanting to put your coach in the middle. Awkward is right. I'm sorry; is there anything we can do to help?"

Beau shook his head. "I just need to tell him I love him. Maybe he'll listen to that."

I leaned over and into the bigger man, draping my arms around him in a hug. "Hang in there. And if you want me to reach out to Damian via FisherFriends under the guise of finding out how he's doing, maybe we can help sort things out."

"Could you?" Beau's dark eyes all but pleaded for the assistance. "Just...I hope he's doing okay. I hope he's enjoying the time with his family. I know he misses his siblings while he's here."

"I'll do the best I can," I promised, and Beau nodded, rising to his feet. "I should leave before Dash kicks me out..."

"I would never!" Dash called out from behind the counter, shaking his finger at Beau. "But if you must leave, I understand. Come back when you need more coffee and another ear."

Beau threw us all a wave and then exited, leaving Owen and I to his lunch, though he had decidedly less time to inhale it now. "Poor guy," I murmured softly, and Owen nodded his agreement as he took a huge bite of his sandwich. "Him and Damian are a bit of an odd couple to begin with, but...they worked. And seemed to genuinely make each other happy."

"When they weren't trying to maim each other," Owen countered. "There's always an underlying layer of tension with those two. Frankly, they probably get off on it, but I imagine with them it's always fighting or epic angry sex."

"Angry sex. Huh." Owen flicked his eyes up to me then winked, making me chuckle. "I don't think we need angry sex. I think we can manage epic without it."

Owen smirked at me. "Keep that up and you're going to have poor Dash gagging behind the counter at the description of our sex life."

"At least you have a sex life!" Dash called back, sighing mournfully. "I launder my cock sock every couple of days now, because it's getting so much use!"

I was very glad I wasn't the one who was eating; I would have spit out my food from laughter. As it was, I nearly wore Owen's sandwich, but he managed to choke it down before he cackled long and hard. "Patience, Dash. Your guy is out there."

"I pray to God every night that is the case. My parents tell me not to worry about this college business, that they will take care of me. But I want independence, to be able to live and love on my own, without their well-meaning but overbearing input."

"They just want what's best for you," I counseled, remembering many long conversations with Dash earlier in the semester at Pride Council. "You are, after all, their first shining light into this new country. They want to keep you in the nest, but remember how proud they were when you sent your midterm grades back to them?"

"I suppose you are right. Everything in good time, yes?" He smiled and wiped down a spot on the counter that didn't exist. "Now, let your poor boyfriend finish his meal so he can get back to work."

"Yes, drillmaster," I teased, and Dash stuck his tongue out at me, not wanting to risk getting caught flipping a customer the bird on the in-store video cameras.

It didn't take too long for Owen to scarf down the rest of his sandwich, and before we left The Big Dough, he stopped at the counter to order some sort of fruity cooled drink concoction. I wasn't even sure what it was called or what it had in it, but Owen seemed excited about it. When we headed on our way, we bid our goodbyes to Dash and headed back to the bookstore.

Unfortunately for me, Owen's lunch break was just about up, so after giving him a kiss outside the store — and outside of camera view — I headed off, with the intention of going back to the apartment and reaching out to Damian. While we got along well enough in Pride Council get togethers, I wasn't sure how he'd react to my inquiring on his well-being. I guess it couldn't hurt to find out.

Once inside the apartment, I changed from my jeans into sleep pants and sat down at our shared desk to open up my laptop. I was going to need to consider dipping into my royalty fund to buy a newer model, which irritated me to no end, but maybe a better investment would be getting Owen a laptop for his birthday in August? It was something to consider at least.

When I finally had a browser window open and FisherFriends loaded, I popped open direct messages, sending Damian a quick note, asking how his spring break was going and if he was planning on going to the next Pride Council meeting once he was back on campus. He'd probably be able to tell I was fishing for information, but what else could I do?

To my great surprise and relief, he answered quickly.

Damian: Hey, Theo! I've been better. Not sure about the meeting. Depends on if I'm in jail for killing my roommate. Ha Ha. :(

Me: Ouch. Things not going well? Anything I can do to help?

Damian: We just...fight. Over the stupidest shit, and then I get so angry with him that I don't even want to see his fucking face. But...I miss him. And I know he's not staying with Pops, which worries me, because he's probably being dense and not taking good care of himself.

Biting lightly on my lip, I was thoughtful in consideration on how to best respond to that. Reveal I'd seen Beau and therefore give up that my inquiry had ulterior motives? Ultimately, I decided against mentioning it.

Me: I can check in on him if you'd like.

Damian: Don't go out of your way to, but if you see him, just make sure he looks fed? Big goofy hockey player. Damn him for having a hold of my heart and my head.

Me: Where am I liable to run into him? He hit any of the campus hot spots on the regular?

Damian: Yeah, The Big Dough. That was actually one of our fights. He and Dash get along so well, I got jealous and he got mad that I didn't trust him, and it just went from there. Like I said, really stupid shit.

Me: To play devil's advocate, I think Dash gets along with everyone really well. It's his usual sunny nature.

Damian: You're right, I know you are. It's just. GAH. Maybe I should come back early. Pops would pick me up. Hell, Mom and Dad would drive me. I'll miss time with the sibs, but summer break is coming up and I can see them then, and I don't know how things are going to work out with Beau over that time. How are you and Owen handling that?

I smiled though he couldn't see it, because while there was no way I'd be able to get to Mystic to visit Owen every weekend, I'd be spending a fair amount of my summer on the Connecticut coastline.

Me: I'll visit him periodically during the summer. It'll be max a three hour drive, so that's doable. I could probably even catch a tour bus to the casinos and then backtrack to Mystic from there.

Damian: That's good, I'm glad for you. Listen though, I think I need to scoot. Someone has made me realize I need to pack and head back to my man. I need him and he needs me. Thank you, Theo.

Me: I didn't do anything but be a friend, Damian. Come visit when you're back in town; maybe we can try cooking you guys something here at the apartment. And maybe we won't set off the smoke alarms this time!
Damian: LOL.

When he signed off, I fist pumped and sent a message to Beau, basically telling him I'd talked with Damian and things were looking up, to just hang in there. I didn't tell him his man was on the way though — I figured that deserved to be a surprise, and I didn't want to ruin it.

My first year at Roseden was quickly coming to a close, but things were looking up. My grades were improving, therapy was helping with my nightmares, and I had Owen.

What more could I ask for?

22

Owen

With school officially over for the year, Theo's parents had come to move us out, though that mostly meant packing up my summer clothes so I'd have things to wear in Mystic. With our apartment staying the same for the next school year, there was no real need to bring anything else home, so beyond my clothes and emptying the fridge out, we were good to go.

Theo's parents had brought a cooler full of food and cold beverages for our four-hour ride to Mystic, and though I was excited, I was also very nervous. While I'd been working jobs as soon as I was old enough to, this was going to be my first adult job. This internship could make or break my career options, and I could feel my anxiety ramping up.

Theo could too. From his seat beside me, he reached over, dragging his thumb down the center of my forehead and whispering, "Relax. Everything is going to be fine." My forehead twitched a little bit but eventually smoothed under his touch, and I sighed softly in his direction.

"I don't want to mess this up."

"You won't," Theo assured me. "You can't, Mr. Four Point Oh. You were made for this internship, and it's going to lead to great things for you. Great things for us." His voice got even softer. "Honestly? I'd even give serious thought to transferring to Mason Island State University so we could live together."

My eyes widened. We always said "for keeps" and meant it, but transferring away from his dream school to follow me? That was intense. "Wow."

He nudged me playfully. "You're stuck with me. You'll have to feed me Boston Creme donuts and lots of coffee; are you prepared for that?"

I sighed melodramatically. "I dunno. That's a lot of pressure." He huffed, and I grinned. "I think I can handle it." Letting my voice dip low, but with lots of growly sex appeal, I whispered in his ear, "There's lots of things I can *handle*."

Theo's ears flushed red and I grinned wide. "I love it when you do," he eventually murmured, and I had the sense that if his mom wasn't constantly sneaking looks into the back seat to watch us, he would have grabbed a handful and squeezed. Even still, he looked tempted to try.

Hooking my arm over his shoulder, I tugged him as close as our seat belts would allow, letting him rest his head on my shoulder. The sigh I made was one of bone deep contentment. "I love having you so close."

"I love being so close," he responded as he turned more towards me, settling so that his hand was over my heart. Could he feel the rhythmic thumping that simple motion caused, I wondered?

Maybe he could, but the only indication of that was the thumb of that hand, sliding back and forth over my heart.

About an hour into our journey and into New York, we stopped at a rest area and pulled out the cooler, settling down at a picnic table in a shady grove to enjoy lunch together. Theo's mom had made sandwiches for everyone, even making roast beef for me to get as close to my beloved steak and cheese as possible. I was touched by the gesture and told her so.

"You're family now, Owen," she offered, and although my initial reaction to such words was wariness, she and Theo's dad meant well. I'd given Theo permission to talk to them about my life and my upbringing, but I wasn't sure how much they'd been made aware of.

"Thank you," I replied softly and dug into the sandwich, knowing that a second one awaited me once I finished the first. Theo watched me as I ate, and I smiled at him from around the sandwich, reaching a hand across the table to cover his.

"You're safe, y'know," he told me, and though my eyes went wide, I kept them locked on him. "They're a little weird; sometimes they don't always say or do the right things, but they do genuinely care."

"Thanks, son," Theo's dad said dryly before turning his attention to me. "He's right though. We do care. We can see how much you love Theo. That means a lot to us. You always worry if your child is going to find a good partner, not just in Theo's case because he's trans, but because the world can be mean-spirited sometimes and not appreciate someone's special qualities. But you can, and you do, and you'll always be welcome in our home because of that."

I lowered my head slightly so they wouldn't see the tears forming in the corners of my eyes; never before had I been in a relationship like this, but more than that, I'd never wanted so badly to be accepted by a family like Theo's. "Thank you," I finally whispered again, unable to summon up any other sort of words.

Theo could see my tears, and he rotated his hand so that he could grab mine and give it a squeeze. I lifted my eyes enough to lock on his again, just staring at him for the longest time, and he had the most serene smile on his face. I'm not sure how long I would have stared at him, but Theo's mom finally broke my trance, saying, "You two are so adorable."

"I've always wanted to be adorable, Mom. Thanks." Theo stuck his tongue out at his mother and then ducked away from her swat, both of them laughing. A smile curled over my lips and I pulled my hand back from Theo's, double fisting my sandwich and resuming devouring it.

A bag of chips appeared and Theo immediately grabbed a handful, but I resisted, not particularly a fan of the way chips made my hands feel after I was done eating them. It was odd, because foods like fried chicken were just as bad for that greasy, salty feeling, but I had no issues with *that*. Maybe I was just weird.

"You're thinking too hard," Theo informed me. "You have that little crease in your forehead again."

"I'll stop thinking," I deadpanned, and everyone laughed, and I took a sip from the can of cola that sat in front of me. But honestly, I didn't need to be thinking about foods with their salt to grease ratio. I needed to just be enjoying my lunch, the companionship of Theo and his family, and the beautiful early summer day. I started to smile, and across the table, Theo's smile widened in response.

When I'd knocked off one sandwich and worked my way through most of the second, I realized that they all were watching me. "You have a healthy appetite," Theo's dad observed.

"I'm a growing boy," I replied, puffing my chest out and laughing again. I was having fun, and I couldn't remember ever having this much fun in an environment like this before. It was scary, yes, but also exhilarating.

Theo met my eye across the table, the faintest hint of a devious twinkle within, and I *knew* he was thinking about a different kind of growing that I did. Well, I *did* do that kind of growing well, too. Especially with him around. But I needed to not be thinking about that with his parents present. That could get awkward.

While I finished my second sandwich, I noticed that they were packing up to go back to the SUV, and I wiped my hands on my shorts, ridding myself of crumbs. When I noticed Theo's mom go to grab the cooler, I intercepted her, telling her with a smile, "Let me."

"Thank you, Owen. You're such a sweet young man."

I'm sure there was a blush coloring my cheeks, but I just carried the cooler to their SUV, putting it near where Theo and I would be sitting for easy access. When he climbed in, out of view of his parents, his hand brushed against the front of my shorts, and my eyes bulged momentarily. "Evil," I whispered to him.

"Nothin' you wouldn't do to me," he countered.

"That is the truth. And just you wait until we're alone together." Making sure my voice was low enough that only he could hear, I reminded him, "I'm going to make you scream so many times your throat'll be raw and you won't be able to walk for a week."

"Promises, promises."

With a quick check to make sure his parents were otherwise occupied, I pressed my hand to the front of his shorts, feeling wetness already pooling through the thin fabric. "Maybe you should ask to stay with me?"

His eyes fluttered shut and he pulled away from me, no doubt to maintain some semblance of dignity. "Tempting. Very tempting. But I don't want you late for your first day of work because I kept you up all night."

Snorting, I moved to buckle myself in one of the seats, waiting until he did the same to grab his hand. "You'd be worth it," I told him sincerely, and the look of pure joy on his face made my heart thump proudly.

With dining out of the way, Theo's dad made the remainder of the drive to Connecticut in good time with plenty of small talk transversing between the seats. His parents were genuinely interested in my internship, what I'd be doing, and the furnished apartment the Seaport had rented me for the summer.

"It's not a huge unit," I explained as we neared the Harbor Heights Apartment Homes, "but not the smallest of their one bedroom units, either. I'm not on the first floor, which makes me happy for safety reasons. I didn't like the idea of people walking by being able to look into my apartment and see what I'm doing."

"Yeah, that is a bit creepy," Theo agreed.

When we finally arrived, we stopped at the main office to pick up keys, and then it was off to park and unpack. My clothes were mostly a mix of comfort clothes, like the shorts I was wearing, and khakis that I'd need for work. I'd probably need to replace my work shoes before the summer was out, but as Theo had been keen to remind me, I *would* be making some decent money this summer.

"Oh, Owen, this place is cute!" Theo's mom cooed as I let us in, and I bit my lip to keep from chuckling.

I'd expected the nautical theme from the pictures on the website, but this was perhaps a bit excessive. For luxury apartments, I wasn't quite expecting to see fish, fake or otherwise, hanging on the wall, but here we were. At least the bedroom looked sizable. Once we had everything put away, I encouraged Theo's parents to sit on the couch while he and I settled on the loveseat. "Thank you, guys, so much for bringing me here. I'm not sure how I would have done it without your help. Maybe had Brent take me to the airport and flown? I don't know..."

"It was our pleasure, Owen," Theo's dad told me. But before I could enjoy their presence too much, he continued, "We should get going though. We've still got another two and a half hours to get home, and the day is getting long in the tooth."

I pouted; I know I did. It was going to be strange not having Theo so close, but at least technology would keep us connected until he could visit. His parents rose to their feet, and his mom pulled me upward as well. When she wrapped her arms around me in a hug, her hand went to my back, putting something in my back pocket. I was startled, but then she patted me and pulled back, telling me, "No looking until we're gone."

Though I was curious, I nodded, and I soon found myself enveloped in a not quite as warm but still friendly hug with Theo's dad. "Be good, son. And let us know if you need anything. That drive is a bit of a hike, but we're here for you if you need us."

I trembled at his words, at the depths of the love behind the offer on the table. It was powerful, and it blew me away that they cared that much. "Thank you," I whispered, all the while trying to keep my emotions in check.

When his parents exited, mumbling something about checking up on Theo in ten minutes if he wasn't in the SUV by that time, I turned to my boyfriend and pulled him close. Burying my face against his neck, I could feel the tears starting to fall, and he made a soft, soothing sound. "It's okay, babe. We'll see each other soon."

"I know, it's just..." I trailed off, at a loss to explain how much losing him scared me. And even though it was only temporary, I wasn't sure how I was going to deal with the separation.

"I know," he whispered as he tilted my face to capture my lips in a kiss, instantly one of possession, tongues sweeping each other's mouths and a soft moan forming in my throat. I pressed my body closer to his, wanting to feel him everywhere, and he purposefully slid his hands beneath my shirt, letting his nails dig into my skin.

"Fuck," I whined. "Don't start that, please. Or I'm not only going to be miserable from missing you, but I'll be hard as a rock."

"Okay." He tapered back his touch, still clinging to me, and we chased each other's tongues again, certainly losing all track of time.

It wasn't until a light knock on the doorframe drew our attention that we stopped kissing, and Theo's mom, blushing madly, tapped on her wrist and gazed at Theo. "It's time."

I sighed and gave Theo one last hug then let him go, eyes following him until he'd closed the door behind himself. It was then that I dropped back to the loveseat, head in my hands as tears streamed unchecked down my face. I was going to miss him terribly, and I hadn't the first clue how to cope with that.

As I sat, though, something poked at my ass, and I remembered Theo's mom sliding something into my shorts. Reaching back, I fished out the object, finding a gift card. My mouth hit the floor when I found the one hundred dollar gift card for the local grocery store, with a note that read, "For staples and things. We love you. The Carters."

If the tears had been streaming before that point, I was outright bawling after. What had I done to deserve them and their love? What had I done to deserve such a sizable gift, sure to get me through the early days of apartment living? I couldn't wrap my head around it at all, and the tears continued.

I managed to pull my cell phone out and send Theo a text, asking him to please thank his parents for their generous gift. And to tell him that I already missed him. He assured me he would and otherwise replied in kind.

It was going to be a long, hard few weeks until I was able to see him again.

Epilogue - Theo

This wasn't the first time I'd come to Mystic to spend time with Owen, but I had big plans for this weekend. Though we continued to tease each other sexually every moment we spent together, we had yet to cross that one final line. I intended to rectify that as soon as the sun set.

For the time being, though, I sat at a chair on Owen's deck, watching him move around the space while he cooked. It still entertained me that my love was now capable of making more than just boxed mac and cheese and was doing so for himself on a regular basis. He was entirely too cheap to go out to eat regularly, so learning to cook had been a task of necessity.

Sniffing the air, I made a happy grunt. Grilled chicken accompanied by grilled vegetables. It was going to be a tasty meal, assuming I left Owen alone long enough that he could concentrate on cooking. "Lookin' good, love," I called out.

He smiled over his shoulder at me. In the few months he'd been in Mystic, he'd lost some of the bulk he'd needed for lacrosse, slimming down slightly. He was still an immense man, capable of squishing me like a bug, but he looked happier than I could ever recall seeing him. "Another few minutes. Could you grab plates from the kitchen?"

Hopping off the chair, I went to do exactly that, already familiar enough with Owen's cabinets to know where everything was. I grabbed silverware while I was at it, putting the knives and forks on the plates for the time being. "Miss me?" I asked as I came back through the sliding door.

"Every moment you're away from me," Owen countered with so much sincerity that it almost hurt my heart. We'd be heading back to school at the end of August, back to our apartment. In a surprising turn of events, Brent had let Owen know he wouldn't be returning, though he wasn't informing the school of that. He and Misha were renting an apartment in Hayboro, where her school, Cordelia Russell College, was based. We hadn't figured out yet if we were going to leave what had been Brent's room set up as a bedroom or arrange it as a computer room for the two of us.

When my parents realized I wanted to buy Owen a new laptop for his birthday, they'd chipped in and helped me research good models for both school work and the type of research work he'd probably be doing in his post-collegiate career. We'd found a good one, upgradable but already pretty powerful, and certainly better than anything Owen had ever used before. I couldn't wait to see his face when he opened that package, but that was another month away.

"Think we're just about done here," Owen informed me. "Plate?" Sliding the silverware onto the table we'd be sitting at, I handed Owen a plate, letting him distribute the food onto it before taking the now filled plate and handing him the empty to repeat the process on. Soon he was joining me at the table, and we smiled at each other before he told me, "I could get used to this."

"Something like you and I in our own place, eating meals we prepped together, living our best lives?" I asked, and Owen nodded between bites of chicken.

"I think this is pretty good, but I'll need your opinion."

I'd been prepping my veggies for devouring but paused that to cut off a piece of chicken, smacking my lips at how tasty and juicy it was. "You did good, babe." He preened at my words, and I leaned across the table to give him a soft kiss. We ate the rest of the meal mostly in silence, only interrupted by soft noises of pleasure as various tastes and flavors hit our mouths.

When we were finished eating, I cleared the table, bringing everything back inside and rinsing off the dishes before loading Owen's dishwasher. Given that it was fairly full from a week of his eating, I got a cleaning tablet from under his sink and started it running, marveling as always at how quiet it was.

Owen came up behind me as I stood in the kitchen, arms around my waist and mouth against my ear, nibbling on my earlobe. I shivered lightly, trying to turn to face him, but his grip was tight enough to keep me where he wanted me. "I was thinking tonight we maybe sit on the deck and watch the fireworks. What say you?"

Feeling him loosen his grip just slightly, I turned to face him, wrapping my arms around his neck and staring up at him with a smile. "I was actually thinking we'd make our own fireworks." As predicted, Owen's eyes darkened at my words, and he even went so far as to lick his lips. "Yeah, I thought you'd like that. I might have even brought the cock ring along." He made a whiny little groan, pulling my body tighter against his, and I could feel his dick starting to awaken in his shorts. "Eager."

"Always with you. And it's only ever you who gets me this hot, this easily. You could walk around with your fingers buried in my ass constantly and I think I'd probably be pretty okay with that. Might be awkward to sit down, but if you kept massaging my prostate I think I'd be too high to notice."

I laughed at him, I couldn't help it, and after a moment he started laughing as well. "Goofball," I told him affectionately, and I brushed my lips against his. He made a low, growly noise and stuck his hands in my back pockets, squeezing my ass through my shorts and making sure that I could feel how very hard he was for me. "You want me to do something about that?" I whispered against his lips.

"Please?" he begged, and there was no way I'd ever deny him anything. Keeping our bodies close together and more or less bouncing off walls, we made it to his bedroom, where there was no delicate strip teases but instead frantic stripping, both of us making it to our underwear in record time.

Looking at him hungrily, I escaped his attempt to grab me and instead went to my bags, burrowing around inside them until I'd pulled out both the cock ring and the strap-on with the "average man" sized dick. Realizing what I was offering, Owen's eyes went wide, and his head nodded like a bobblehead, silently pleading for me to continue.

Pausing near his window, I closed the shades most of the way, but left them open just enough we'd be able to see the sky lit up later. Then I turned my attention back to Owen, helping him out of his boxer briefs. Nuzzling his cock with my face and hearing him whine, I carefully snapped the cock ring into place, stroking him a few times to make him pant for breath.

"Why don't you get on the bed. Put a pillow under your ass." He didn't need to be told twice; he was off and moving, getting himself comfortable on the bed and gazing at me hungrily. "I'm tempted to tease you and suck you before I fuck you. But that might just be mean, given your current situation."

"You're trying to make sure I pass out from this orgasm, aren't you?" Owen asked, and I just grinned at him. He made a low moan and I did crawl up between his legs, nuzzling his dick once more before taking the head into my mouth, my hand coming up to stroke him ever-so-slowly.

While he mumbled nonsensically, I kept up the attention on his dick, stroking and sucking, sucking and stroking, knowing I was driving him wild and there wasn't a damn thing he could do about it. When he started to beg for mercy, I gave him some and backed off, letting him calm down.

With Owen catching his breath, I set about assembling the strap-on, pleased that the one I'd chosen had stimulation for me as well. Once I was ready to go, I grabbed the lube I'd brought for this occasion and slicked up my fingers, bringing one to trace around the edge of Owen's hole. He whined immediately, his legs spreading wider to give me greater access, and I loved the look of him opening up for me.

I worked a single finger past the tight ring of muscle, plunging it deep until I could bump his prostate, hearing him cuss so pretty when I did so. I worked him up pretty good with that single finger, but it was when I folded in the second finger that I thought his brain was going to explode.

"Goddamn fuckity shit," he cussed, and I almost giggled despite myself. I could see he was getting overheated, though, so I stilled my hand, just watching him until his breathing slowly, oh so slowly, went back to something akin to normal. Once it did, I rubbed his prostate again, and he begged, "Fuck me, please. I need you so badly."

Only too happy to oblige, I slathered up the very realistic looking dildo with lube, edging the head into his hole as he hissed slightly. He probably could have used more prep, but I understood his desperation. It hadn't been that long ago that he'd made me walk crooked for several days after getting me off over and over again with his mouth and fingers.

Once he relaxed, I pushed in further until I was fully sheathed, and it was then I began to thrust, feeling the strap-on grind against my dick, making it my turn to drop the f-bombs. Leaning over top of him and trying to get close enough to kiss him,

I buried myself in his ass over and over again until I could see his eyes rolling back in his head. It was at that point that I shifted my balance to free his dick from the cock ring, and he exploded untouched, crying out so loudly that I was certain his neighbors heard him.

I kept thrusting until I felt my own orgasm build and then wash over me, shuddering as I collapsed on top of him just as the fireworks started outside. Nuzzling against his neck, I whispered to him, "Love you."

It took him several minutes to come back down to earth, to catch his breath, but when he did, it was with a strongly voiced, "Love *you*." He took another deep breath and then added on, "Fuck that was amazing. You controlling my orgasm like that? Any time of the day, babe."

Carefully pulling out of him and undoing the strap-on, I eventually rolled back on top of Owen, kissing open-mouthed across his face until our lips locked and we shared wet, hungry kisses. Our bodies rubbed against each other, getting us both hot all over again, and I could see it was going to be one of those nights.

Not that I would ever complain about being loved on by Owen. There was no better feeling in the world.

FIN

Want to see what the future has brought Theo and Owen? Check out the free bonus story, "For Keeps", exclusively available by scanning the below QR code.

Did you enjoy this book? Reviews are always appreciated. Please scan the QR code below to leave one.

Also By Shayne Prescott

The Roseden University universe starts with ***Blind Disaster***. You can get it **FREE** on BookFunnel (newsletter opt-in required). Scan the QR code to download it.

About Shayne

Shayne Prescott has been putting together books since his medium was scraps of paper and pencil nubs. A children's book was considered for publication while in middle school, and his short stories were often a favorite of his beloved English teacher, Mrs. Mazzacarro. Still, he writes.

Website

Newsletter

Facebook

Amazon

Goodreads

Patreon

Made in the USA
Middletown, DE
25 January 2022